SLAVES

SLAVES

by

William Maltese

The Borgo Press
An Imprint of Wildside Press

MMVII

CHAPTER 1

The space in the first-class restroom, on the flight from Johannesburg to Dar Es Salaam, was cramped. It helped that the young flight attendant had fucked there before. Timothy knew right where to stand to advantage what little space he had. His pants (he wore no undershorts), were dropped around his ankles. His large cock and large accompanying balls, the latter within their containing sac of blond-haired skin, were propped upon the leading lip of the cool porcelain sink.

He handed a condom packet to the young man positioned directly behind him.

"By the look of that long-lasting boner in your trousers, I decided 'Large' was your size," Timothy said. "Lubricated, because it's been a long time since my butt ate such a hefty meal."

He put one hand to each vertical edge of the mirror and waited for Jack Mallard to unveil the hard cock Timothy had anticipated since the beginning of the flight.

Jack was made hot by the twin globes of Timothy's bare buttocks flattened slightly along their mutually shared crack. He could have just unzipped, yanked out his stiff prick, socked it with latex, and shoved it right in. However, he had a bit more control than first-impulse. It wasn't as if he were a virgin, egged on by the misconception that if he didn't get "It" now, hard and fast, an opportunity might never again present itself. Nor was he a novice, as far as fucking in the lavatory of a plane. His job had taken him through a helluva lot of airways round the world, and had initiated him into, as he had initiated others into, more than one of the 10,000-feet and 20,000-feet "fuck clubs." Sometimes, like now, he even fucked in the air lanes for free.

For fun. Thank God he could still enjoy sex outside the dollars and cents of it!

Jack dropped his pants and underpants to join the puddle of Timothy's clothing at the young men's feet. He did so not only to avoid whatever sweat stains Timothy's luscious ass would have eventually painted on Jack's trouser crotch, but because Jack always enjoyed the feel and sound of bare ass against his bare belly, especially in those last moments of a fuck when it really took off.

Jack's cock enjoyed its freedom. It had been cramped, no end, within the dark confinement of his slacks. It advantaged its release by swelling even larger. Its cockhead ballooned its pulpy surface to reveal the pee-hole that punctuated a lengthy groove that almost halved the meaty knob. Circumcision scar formed a slightly discolored collar of skin just beneath the impressive mushroom flaring of the cockhead. Below that collar, the rest of the cockneck curved downward, flattened along its back and belly to provide a tube of stiff meat whose circumference was more elliptic than round, whose impressive length was more bow than straight-arrow. The thick cockroot, more than even Jack's massive hand-span could ever completely circumvent, anchored within a black tangle of curly, pubic hair. Dangling from that cockroot was a fist-sized scrotum that was already desire-yanked into a compact, elevated, and hair-covered mass of shifting skin.

Jack momentarily dealt with the aluminum packet, and its lubricated condom, by holding the former in his teeth while he rolled the tail of his shirt and undershirt upward into a secure tuck that revealed his stomach and chest, all of the way to his already taut and dime-sized nipples. Above the triangle of his thick sexual bush, his abdominals, defined as surely as any antique washboard, had less and less fur as they neared the small halo of strands that emphasized the indent of his navel.

When his stomach finally gave way, it was to the nearly complete hairlessness of his well-delineated pecs.

In ready anticipation, Jack's cock was jerked by a spasm controlled by muscles deep within his groin. Jack's cockhead thumped into actual meeting with his muscled belly. The resulting "Slap!" was audible and knocked a splattering of sticky clear juice from his cockmouth. The resulting liquid caught and beaded within the hair that haloed Jack's navel. Meanwhile, excess leakage drooled the belly of Jack's cock and would have provided more than ample lubricant had the fuck been scheduled without any readily oiled protective condom.

Jack, though, wasn't about to proceed without latex protection. After all, this was Africa, wasn't it? "They" said AIDS might have originated somewhere within the Dark Continent. From monkeys, maybe, swinging in the trees of the night-dark forest below.

His shirttail rolled and secured, his cock wiped dry with toilet tissue, Jack ripped off one end of the aluminum condom wrapping, using his teeth. He leaned back against the wall that, due to the confinement in which the two young men played, was only a few inches away. It was far enough away, though, for him to dispense with the condom wrapper, into the wastebasket, pinch the nose of the lubricated latex, in order to provide ample room for the eventual deluge of cum soon to be filling it from Jack's cum-bulged balls, and hat the tip of his prick with the nipple-nose rubber. The dark red color of the latex turned pink against the dark neck of his cock, as the rubber was rolled down the entire length of his erection. Jack's guiding fingers pressed the finally released lower ovaling of the condom to be sure that it firmly gripped the hairy root of his cock.

"I'm getting hotter and hornier as I stand here," Timothy said and anticipated what was coming. If the only part of Jack the mirror reflected, for Timothy's viewing pleasure, was Jack's handsome face, Timothy didn't need the seeing to know what he had here. He'd made an art of spotting male passengers and knowing what existed beneath the conventional covering of their travel clothes. He'd known right off, the second Jack stepped on board in Johannesburg, that here was a young man, hardly older than Timothy, who had it all. And Timothy wanted it all, or at least all of one particular part of Jack, rammed up Timothy's asshole so far Timothy's butt would be flattened by the push of the entry.

Jack's hands went to Timothy's waist, then slid down to the young man's hips. Jack's thumbs hooked the matching globes of Timothy's ass and pulled outward to reveal the depth of the awaiting hair-lined crack.

"Looks tight," Jack said. He had leaned in to make it a whisper against Timothy's ear. Saying it "looks tight" was as far as he was going to go, for the moment. He knew, from experience, that looks could be deceiving. Even Timothy's small pucker might provide little or no resistance, opening into a barn-like cavern so used and abused that there might hardly be enough friction for adequate orgasm. After all, Jack had no doubt that Timothy had been in this position before. Timothy had simply been too expert in letting Jack know of his availability, and following up on it, not to have thoroughly honed his skills at passenger seduction.

Timothy read Jack's mind. "If anything, my asshole is tighter than it looks," he promised with a smile. "Believe it or not, I'm usually not the one leaned over the sink."

That possibly the case, the notion made Jack's dick leak more sticky goo inside its rubber. Jack felt the latest oozing and had to be careful. Back in the pre-AIDS days, his cock's tendency to self-lubricate would have been a decided advantage. It would have meant no need for supplemental KY, or Vaseline, or soap, or whatever, to let his cock slip inside the tightest ass. In this day and age, though, it meant being damned sure his cock didn't get so juiced up that it prematurely slipped out of whatever rubber sheathe was draped to protect it.

Jack lined up his cockhead, made seemingly longer by the condom's tented nipple, to the inviting pucker that pouted Timothy's asscrack. Jack pushed his hips slowly forward and nudged his rubber-cloaked cockhead directly to the doorway.

"Knock, knock," Jack said. His mouth was back on Timothy's ear. He smelled Timothy's pleasant after-shave and wondered what brand it was. He looked up and saw, in the mirror, that Timothy's right hand was no longer on the reflecting surface but wrapped around Timothy's erect cock jutted up from the lip of the sink.

"I can take care of that truncheon for you," Jack volunteered.

"You just concentrate on the fucking," Timothy instructed. "This truncheon and I go back a long ways, and I know just what it likes while the likes of you drill my backside."

"Mmmmm," Jack offered in ready compliment and ran his hands forward around Timothy's hard stomach, then up beneath the young man's shirt. He felt Timothy's two hard nipples, and he paused to pinch each to an even greater hardness. Finally, though, he curved his arms up the front of Timothy's body and locked his hands, one up and over each of Timothy's shoulders.

Jack paused, one moment longer, merely enjoying a voyeur's pleasure in seeing what was reflected back to him from the mirror. Timothy was one good-looking and young stud. But, then, Jack had always been a sucker for blond hair, blue eyes, and pouty lips. Timothy's cock was an excitement in its own right. Uncircumcised and fat, it might, in Jack's humble opinion, warrant some experimentation, later, up Jack's own butt. Maybe, if time allowed.

"Yes, fuck my butt! Oh, yes!" Timothy greeted the pressure that concaved the center of his asspucker and sent the entrance of his asshole into even wider expansion, as if his pucker were the lens of a camera. Then, as if converted into a miniature mouth, his asspucker suddenly had its gumming lips rolled up and over the pulpy cockhead that Jack continued to feed it.

"Sweet, sweet ass," Jack enjoyed. Inside the asshole, as far as the flaring of his cockhead, his cockneck experienced a vise-like pressure from the snug ass that now, agape, firmly anchored on circumcision scar tissue. "You didn't lie buddy, when you said 'tight,' did you?"

"My mom always told me not to lie about anything easily proven false," Timothy said. He exerted the backward pressure that sank the next inch of Jack's hard cock up Timothy's asshole.

"Well, let me tell you something that isn't a lie," Jack said and put yet another inch of his cock inside. "I'm going to fuck you within an inch of your life."

"Promises," Timothy said, simultaneous with the steady slide that buried all that was left of Jack's cock up Timothy's behind. As a result, Timothy's voice emerged more than a little breathless.

"I am a man of my word," Jack promised and slapped his crotch firmly into a squashing of Timothy's butt that ground Jack's hard cock up Timothy's asshole: human pestle gyrating within human mortar.

Timothy arched his neck, the long line of it presenting his Adam's apple to a more prominent view that played out well in the reflection of the mirror. He gave his big cock exactly five rapid, piston-like pumps, with his fist. Then, he stopped and held tight while his erection swelled larger and pried open his grip even farther. His cock had a heartbeat its very own. At the same time, the whole corridor of Timothy's plugged butt rippled in muscular contractions, like a snake attempting to feed a recently swallowed meal to the digestive juice of its belly.

It took all of Jack's conscious control to slow the spiralling pleasure Timothy's anal tremors provided Jack's butt-wrapped cock. Only when he literally reminded himself that he wasn't a rank amateur at this, hardly someone to blow his wad after only a few seconds of delightful penetration, was Jack able to abort those impulses that threatened, prematurely, to explode his sperm, right then and there.

"Something tells me you're going to be really good," Timothy decided. Not unaware of his own expertise, he could genuinely be complimentary, now that it was obvious that he had finally lucked onto someone who might not only match his own skills in the intricacies of the sexual dance but actually surpass them. He'd not been wrong to offer up his ass to this young stud; he knew that before they went even one second farther. Thank God for that insightful intuition which had, this time, told Timothy to drop his pants, and bare his firm ass, because that same intuition told him he was in for one hell of a ride. Likewise, he was determined that Jack came away from this with the knowledge that butt-plugging Timothy's tight rectum, in a jet airliner probing, in its own phallic way, the night-dark skies over Southeast Africa, was an experience to be given very high marks even among the pro ranks of fucking.

Just how tight a fit it was, that cock up that butt, was illustrated by Timothy's, "Wait just ... one ... moment ... more," when Jack first attempted to dislodge some of the engorged stuffing. For a moment, Timothy's bowel was so seemingly snug, around the fully probed piece of phallic meat, his rectum seemed at risk of turning inside-out should Jack succeed in any immediate withdrawal. On the other hand, it didn't take more than the requested moment for Timothy's butthole to relax just that extra bit so, what with the lubricant already left on the asshole lining by the entering condom, Timothy no longer risked disembowelment.

"Now, stud!" Timothy invited, his butt truly ready for its fuck. He gave a roll of his behind that torqued Jack's cock partially free before screwing it right back into place.

"More than ready, you tight-assed, handsome bastard," Jack said. He pulled back his muscled stomach from its meeting with Timothy's muscled butt. The drag of rubber-sheathed prick, up tight asshole, made the pucker of Timothy's ass convex with the friction. It remained convex as Jack dragged his dick out to the rim formed by the flaring of his cockhead. The pucker went concave only on the inward thrust that returned Jack's hard meat so far up Timothy's eagerly awaiting butt that the black hair on Jack's crotch met with, and entangled with, the blond strands that lined the musky depths of Timothy's asscrack.

"Yes, yes, yes," Timothy invited. There was no pain as Jack's cock gave a repeat performance: out to its cockhead, in to its root, out yet again.

Meanwhile, Jack used all the expertise he'd ever garnered as a top-man to continue the rise of pleasure this tight fuck of Timothy's seemingly virgin ass was providing. It took a good deal of concentration not to give in to the pleasure and proceed into gone-out-of-control pumping of cock up butt. Of course, Jack knew that by delaying his orgasm he would benefit himself, not to mention benefit Timothy. Delay layered pleasure upon pleasure. Stacked it precariously, like a house of cards. The more cards stacked, the more to tumble when orgasmic earthquake finally came.

At moments, though, during the ensuing fuck, even Jack, with his knowledge of the do and don't of any lengthy and pleasurable fucking, felt he was on the verge of losing control.

At such times, he paused, usually with his cock fully buried. Any pause with even part of his cock outside the asshole, and he risked a backward thrusting of Timothy's butt in unwanted and final stimulus to orgasm. Even as it was, his prick completely stuck, Jack was provided with a sensual roll of Timothy's hips, and a clamping and undulating anal massage courtesy of Timothy's bowel. Both of which required Jack to refocus his total attention on stacking — Oh, yes, please God! — one more pleasure card.

During one phase, Timothy took advantage and revised his position at the sink. He stepped out of his left shoe, pulled his left foot up through his puddled clothes. He bent his left leg at its knee and elevated that knee to the point where his foot was placed firmly on the edge of the sink, not that far from his cock. With little more effort, he rested his chin on his knee. His left hand dropped downward, beneath his overhanging ass, then farther behind. His fingers found Jack's balls, claimed them, and gave them a massaging squeeze.

"Sweet Jesus!" was Jack's immediate response. No doubt that the sensuous ache, provided by Timothy's suddenly kneading fingers, around Jack's cum-bulged testicles, helped keep Jack's orgasm at bay for a little while longer. Then again, the pain was a pleasure, in and of itself, that stacked even more cards into the house of pleasure; that house now precariously close to its final and ultimate destruction.

Timothy had periodically pumped his fat erection, in a tempo that perfectly added only those additional spurts of pleasure the young man could endure without, himself, spilling over the brink into orgasm. Now, he gave his handful of cock a few more careful up and down torques, his velvety foreskin rolling down to shoot his cockhead to impressive visibility. His fisted fingers then dragged the very same loose skin back up his cockneck to hide his cockhead, as if his cockhead were a monk's head suddenly draped by priestly cowl.

Unlike Jack's cock, Timothy's prick wasn't a leaker. Its layer of lubricating dampness was provided exclusively by the spit Timothy periodically spat into the palm of his right hand and, then, smeared along his swollen erection.

Timothy's cockhead was bright red. Its skin, stretched to its limits by engorged blood, was as taut as any red balloon blown to full capacity.

Jack began another pull of his dick. When the movement threatened to pull his balls free of Timothy's massaging fingers, he paused briefly, and Timothy let go. Jack's scrotum, when freed, was a compact mass of wrinkled, hair-covered skin, hefted so close to the thick base of his prick that his balls threatened their complete disappearance into those very cavities from which they'd initially dropped at the onset of puberty. Nonetheless, when his cock plowed back up Timothy's butt, his balls immediately returned to Timothy's awaiting hand and to an additional series of sensuous squeezes.

In gauge of Timothy's elevating pleasure, Timothy's scrotum, like that of Jack's, no longer hung freely. It, too, was compact and elevated to seeming disappearance. Timothy, though, didn't need that particular sign to tell him he was flying so high that he was about to run out of fuel. Better warning was the electrical jolt that physically shook him each and every time Jack's butt-fucking cock poked Timothy's swollen prostate and slid deeper. Another jolt occurred as the same cockhead bounced back across Timothy's prostate as Jack's prick returned to free a good length of itself from Timothy's asshole.

"I'm getting mighty hot and bothered, stud," Jack said. He didn't know if he talked to Timothy, or talked to his own flustered face as reflected by the mirror.

There was something exciting about Jack's darkly tanned countenance grown exotically darker beneath his sexual blush, as contrasted with the obvious pink that presently tinged Timothy's usually peaches-and-cream complexion. Had the skin of Timothy's chest and belly been seen, beneath its present drapery of his shirt, it, too, would have been revealed as tinged an attractive rose.

"Tell me when you're going to blow," Timothy insisted. No doubt that he would cum at one and the same time: a miracle in itself, but even more so in that he would get there without any additional pumps of his cock. All his keyed-up senses, to be set over the edge, needed only Jack's hot and heavy cum exploded into the nippled condom that rode the friction-heated corridors of Timothy's butt.

"I want you to cum, too, you sexy bastard," Jack notified, although he was too far gone to exert any additional control needed to keep his peaking pleasure at bay.

"You're going to get your wish," Timothy promised. "Make yours fast, and we might even ... ah ... ah ... Jesus, I'm ... going ... to ..."

"Jesus, I'm ..." Jack could only echo. He plugged his cock one final time into Timothy's oh-so-tight and massaging asshole

Their combined, "Aaaghrraahhhh!" was so coordinated, it came out as two-part harmony.

By the looks and feel, it could have been Jack's wads of spunk, forcefully exploded through protective rubber, and pulsed, in wet-white streamers, up through and out of Timothy's spewing erection. In fact, though, Jack's cum, despite its tremendous heat and volume, was stopped and contained by the pink condom nipple now so stuffed with cum that it added a good inch to Jack's butt-fucked erection. The cum that whipped out of Timothy's dick was all his. There was so much of it that streamers of it caught and hung not only to the mirror, not only to the soap dispenser, not only to both faucets, but even to the wall.

CHAPTER 2

There was nothing about their perfunctory good-byes, unless it was each young man's knowing grin, that said Jack and Timothy had spent a good deal of their in-flight time having wild and crazy sex in the first-class restroom. Nor did the stewardess, stationed with Timothy at the open door of the plane that gave access to the airport terminal at Dar Es Salaam, have any kind of smirk that said she was aware — or, at least, gave a damn — as to what the young male attendant and young male passenger had been up to

Jack's connecting flight to Zanzibar was nowhere as enjoyable as the one with Timothy on board.

After having checked into his Zanzibar hotel, he strolled the hotel driveway to where it merged with Creek Road. The latter's name was a misnomer, because there was no creek to offer coolness. The ocean, to rear and right, offered no respite, in that it was blocked by the hotel and the town.

The temperature was too hot and too humid to risk being anywhere in it without a hat. Jack knew that. Even pretending that he was dim-witted enough to forget, made him feel a little ridiculous. However, he was being paid more than enough for the inconvenience to his pride, so ...

He finally located the lone sapling and its pitiful offering of super-heated shade. He plopped down into the latter and checked his watch.

On schedule, the bicycle appeared, headed in his direction.

Jack attempted to look as if he suffered from borderline heatstroke. Not too difficult to do.

In a few minutes, the bike was alongside, its rider recognizable from photos Jack had been shown.

– 13 –

"My God, young man!" greeted Carl Mider, right on cue. "Didn't anyone tell you that you shouldn't step outside, here, even for a moment, without something covering your head?!"

Anyway, Jack surmised that was what Carl said, according to pre-written script. Since Carl had said it in Swedish, Jack really couldn't be sure.

"Sorry, I only speak English," Jack said.

"Brit?" Carl asked, this time in English and in well-feigned ignorance.

"American."

"Then, it can't be the old saw about only mad dogs and Englishmen out in the midday sun, can it?" Carl said. "Here ..." and he unzipped the flight bag within the wire basket attached to his bicycle's handlebars. "I come equipped with extra headgear."

He produced and handed over one of those Australian bush hats, bent up on one side and pinned to its crown.

"Why don't I bike you to my place for a bit of liquid refreshment out of this bloody sun?" Carl suggested. It was just the bonhomie expected from one foreigner to another, the one cognizant of his surroundings, the other obviously at a loss.

Even before straddling his tight ass over the bike's rear fender, Jack had taken good stock of Carl Mider and decided the man's photograph hadn't done Carl justice. The flesh-and-blood Carl was loads better looking, although no denying Carl came stamped with those bookish good looks so often associated with people in "the sciences".

Carl's tortoise-shell glasses, the lenses of which emphasized his pale blue eyes, only enhanced his air of academia. On the other hand, his tousled blond hair, or what Jack could see of the few loose strands that appeared beneath the "Redskins" baseball cap backward-anchored on Carl's head, was downright boyish. Carl's small nose, and too-thin lips, completed the picture of someone more apt to be seen as attending college, than being a member of the faculty. But, then, looks could deceive. Carl was highly respected, not only as a practicing doctor of medicine, but as someone whose botanical research into the potential of obscure medicinal plants had been recognized as first-class by publication in some very prestigious medical journals.

As there were no hand-grips for riding tandem, Jack rested his hands gently around Carl's waist. What his fingers gently enfolded was as solid as rock. Carl's doing a lot of his research in the field kept him in A-one shape, an exception to some really physically active men Jack knew who still battled "the bulge" and attending "love handles". Not that Carl, if ugly as a stump, or out of shape as any long-time couch potato, would have made a stick of difference to Jack. However, it was a decided bonus to have it otherwise.

Expertly, Carl pedalled them down Creek Road to where it passed the marketplace of low sheds filled with fruit, fly-swarmed fish, meat, poultry and people. Anyone who looked their way seemingly paid little attention; strange in that there were so very few foreigners on Zanzibar since the revolution.

The bike swerved right and proceeded to a complete and balanced stop.

The riders dismounted, and Carl led the way up the front steps of the museum.

An old Negro stood at the open front door.

"Jasper," Carl greeted.

Jasper nodded as both men walked by.

The dim-lit interior was hotter than the out-of-doors.

Carl guided Jack around several glass cases and stopped at one.

"Can you think of a more appropriate nest for a doctor of medicine than the one containing the medical papers of the one and only Dr.-Livingstone-I-presume?"

He led the way to a humidity-warped door that opened no more easily than the equally distorted doors Jack had left at his hotel.

Carl ushered Jack on through.

"Nothing plush, but it's livable," Carl defined. "Actually, it's downright palatial if you consider some of the other places I've stayed." It was small and cluttered but invited with a bit of cool air that entered through one of several open windows. "Please don't stand on formality, but have a seat on the bed. My lone chair, I'm afraid, requires a balancing act to keep it from collapsing at each sitting."

Jack sat on the cot.

Carl shut the door and leaned back against it to provide extra assurance it had completely closed.

"We can talk freely here," Carl said, focused exclusively on his guest. "Even if the government had access to sophisticated listening devices (and from all I can learn, they don't), it's doubtful they could afford them. So, please tell me that Field wasn't lying when he said that if your job-position called for it, you'd fuck a horse, or willingly be fucked by one."

"You have a particular horse in mind?"

"Actually, I have myself in mind. Although, horse-like is a misnomer. No point in pretending otherwise. My dick is only a mere seven inches in erection. Do you know how long it's been, though, since those seven inches have had a decent fuck of a butt?"

"According to my sources, you've been in Africa for about two years. A year and a half on the mainland, helping out at some 'barefoot doctor' clinic, sponsored by the Swedish government; the last six months, here, on Zanzibar. But, surely, somewhere along the line, you had some play-time with a fellow Swede, or with some of the local talent."

"Twice, as far as fellow Swedes go," Carl admitted. "They are, after all, the only group of foreigners who've truly discovered the tourist bargain Zanzibar is. Zilch, though, by way of counting my sexual adventures with the indigenous population. Homosexuality is against the law here, isn't it?!. Which is why I insisted Field send a courier who was gay. The last thing I want, after having devoted the last two years of my life to this project, is to blow it (pardon the double entendre) by getting caught, flagrante delicto, with some local stud's big, fat, black whanger stuck in one or the other of my body orifices."

Still, Jack suspected that the rewards for Carl's abstinence, based upon how much Jack was being paid for just his participation, would be more than enough to offset whatever the inconvenience for Carl's temporary removal from the sexual mainstream.

"First things first, though," Carl said. "You do look as if you could use a drink, or is that just an excellent act?"

"I could use a drink," Jack admitted.

"One drink, coming up," Carl promised. He headed toward a pile of newly-harvested coconuts in one corner and scooped up one which he carried to a nearby sideboard. He picked up a machete, held the coconut over a wide-rimmed bucket and sliced off the top of the nut, without spilling a drop of the liquid interior. He put the machete to one side and brought Jack the decapitated results. He went to a cupboard, nailed precariously to one wall, and he opened one cupboard door. "Sorry I didn't offer you at least a share of my last bottle of Coke," he apologized and produced the bottle in question, "but I've become less and less hospitable as my days here drag on."

He pried off the bottle cap with the lower edge of the machete blade. The warm pop fizzed and overflowed, but he quickly anchored his thin lips sensuously over the phallic top of the bottle to contain the explosion. He came to the chair,

– 17 –

positioned near where Jack sat, and carefully eased his firm butt into the seat.

Jack took another swallow of the surprisingly refreshing contents of the opened shell.

"This is what gets mainly thrust up my butt these days." Carl lifted the Coke bottle so there was no missing his insinuation. "It's prime advantage: it never gets soft, always erect when I'm hot to trot. As to what I fuck, I resort mainly to what you now have in hand."

Jack paused mid-swallow.

Carl laughed. He had a pleasant laugh that went well with his boyish but bookish good looks.

"Oh, not that particular coconut," Carl assured. "But, to be sure, a whole variety of its brothers, fathers, cousins, and uncles. Each made amiable by the mere drilling of a strategically placed hole, here or there, measured to certain anatomically specific dimensions."

"I'd like to see you fuck a coconut," Jack said and wasn't lying. Just the idea of Carl's seven-inch cock working back and forth, back and forth, inside a nut, while the coconut water, inside, sloshed around Carl's pumping penis, was enough to give Jack an erection.

"Except, I'm tired of fucking coconut," Carl reminded. "Why don't I fuck you, instead?"

"Why not?" Jack said with a shrug. It had been his experience that sex with guys who had been without, for long periods, was usually a pretty satisfying experience. Especially when Jack was being paid so well to do it. "However, how about my fucking a coconut while I'm getting my ass screwed by you?"

"I've a Swahili class in ..." Carl checked his watch. "Oh, hell, why not?"

Carl got up, went back to the sideboard, where he folded a

piece of aluminum foil into a thin strip.

He brought the result to Jack.

"Pull out that cock of yours and use this to wrap your pecker's thickest part," Carl instructed. "I'll see what I can do for you in the little time allotted."

If Jack had difficulty complying, it was only because he went for his cock through his open zipper, and his prick was already so swollen that it didn't want to provide even the slight bend necessary to be fished on through. Finally, he just undid his pants and let them drop, his undershorts along with them.

"Jesus!" Carl admired. "If you and that hard, beautiful cock of yours aren't a sight for these sore eyes."

Jack used the aluminum foil to mold a record of his cock's thickest circumference, and he handed the result over to Carl who went back to the sideboard with it. Carl retrieved a fresh coconut from the existing pile, and he used the aluminum circle to gauge the size of the hole he was about to drill.

He put the coconut into a readily available vise which was, also, used for more official chores. He produced a hand drill, with suitable bit.

Unlike any coconut found in US grocery stores, this came directly off the tree and retained the green-colored husk that provided several inches of highly compact fiber before the dark, more readily recognizable, hard shell that was lined with its creamy white fruit. Coconut water, and far more of it than was ever found in any grocery-store sold nut, filled the center.

Jack could tell by the easy flow of the procedure that Carl had, in fact, had a lot of practice doing what he was doing. As the coconut became more and more ready for Jack's cock, Jack became more and more aroused by the prospect of fucking it. He'd been around the block so many times that he was always excited when something new appeared on his horizon.

Carl finished his chore with a small file.

Slaves

"Wouldn't want any rough edges to damage that impressive hunk of meat of yours," Carl said, and eyed his workmanship, which, although not as perfect as he would have liked it, was going to have to make-do, considering the diminishing time element.

Students enrolled at the Zanzibar Institute of Swahili Language Studies were supposed to be more interested in scholastics than in anything, and the teachers took tardiness, and/or unpreparedness for any lesson, as indication that dedication was lacking. More than one lackadaisical man and woman had been dismissed as a result. As Carl's enrollment had been hard-won, and continued as part of his cover for being on Zanzibar, it was important he retain his good rapport with Institute personnel.

"You want to try this on for size?" Carl asked, only because he figured Jack and he still had the time.

However, before he handed over the drilled nut, he used a felt-tipped pen to draw two eyes and a nose on the outside husk. The hole he'd worked into the nut now seemed the eager mouth of a green-headed, want-to-suck-your-cock alien.

"Meet Cory Coconut," Carl introduced. "Try not to lose any of the liquid sloshing inside Cory's throat. Wet makes for a far better fuck — doesn't it always? — than a dry-fuck. Speaking of wet, maybe a bit of extra lubricant is called for, since I'm not sure I didn't make the fit a tad snug. I just happen to have some cocoa butter." He produced a can. "Better yet, why not let me give you the lube?"

Jack stood, and Carl dropped to his knees before Jack's impressive erection.

"Hold the coconut, just for the moment, will you, stud?" Carl requested. Once free of the nut, he scooped cocoa butter from the can and proceeded to smear Jack's boner with it. "Damn, but I can't believe I'm actually manhandling real, genuine, hard-as-a-rock American-male prick."

A thick lubrication completed, Carl requested the return of the coconut, which he tilted until its inside juices made their appearance at the opening of its mouth. He took a new hold of Jack's cock, as if, this time, he laid claim to a large switch that, when engaged, would connect him to some major power grid: which was, indeed, the case. He tugged the cock from its stalwart, upright position, to one that was more parallel the floor. He put Jack's cockhead directly to the tilted coconut mouth.

"Time to fuck Cory Coconut," Carl said. Jack was only too eager to oblige with a forward bucking at the very same time Carl shifted the nut for a more perfect alignment of lubricated prick to provided hole. Jack's boner slid through the breach, only a bit of the nut's liquid, and a bit of the cocoa butter, getting free to catch within the black pubic hair along Jack's lower belly.

"Feels cool," Jack said. He meant that literally and figuratively. The insulating shell of any fresh-from-its-tree coconut was what always made its water, even within a nut come directly from sunlight, pour out thirst-quenchingly cool.

"Cory's one lucky nut!" Carl said and got to his feet. "I'm jealous, but not for long."

Jack watched Carl strip, delighted by what he saw. Just as he'd surmised, Carl's stomach was completely absent of fat. So much so that Carl's hipbones were prominent, his belly slightly concave without being unattractively so. Except for the blond-hair of his pubic bush, and the tousled blond strands on his head, Carl came across seemingly hairless. His muscle definition, and it was readily visible, wasn't the bas-relief of a body-builder but more etched, like fine lines exquisitely inscribed on gold leaf.

Yes, Jack might well have fucked a horse, or been fucked

by one, if that were part of his job description. However, there was no doubt that getting fucked by someone like Carl, in substitute, made it all the more easy for Jack's ecstasy to come across genuine, from the very outset. One thing, though. If Jack ever fucked Carl belly-up, or was fucked belly-up by the man, he'd ask Carl to remove those eyeglasses. While some people's looks were definitely improved by glasses, Carl was someone who would have looked far more attractive without them. As it was, Carl prepared to mount Jack from behind, it really didn't matter whether or not Carl kept his glasses on or not, since Jack wouldn't be looking at him.

There was, however, one final thing which had to be taken care of before any serious fucking began.

"You have a rubber, or do you want one of mine?" Jack queried.

"Good question." Carl decided. "It having been so long since I've fucked a real person, coconuts hardly ever insisting upon protection. How about we use one of yours? I do have a supply, but the wretched climate around here has been known to do as strange things to latex as it has done to people."

"There's one in the right front pocket of my shirt."

"I do like a young man who comes prepared," Carl said. "While we're on the subject of your shirt, why don't you let me help you slip it off? You've got way too nice a body to keep it even partially covered."

When they were both completely naked, except for Carl's glasses, Carl rolled the rubber over his total seven inches. The prophylactic was a black one which made it amusingly apropos for black Zanzibar.

Satisfied that Carl was correctly outfitted for fucking, Jack turned his enticing butt in Carl's direction. Both Jack's hands held to Cory Coconut in such a way as to make it appear as if his fingers cupped an alien's ears. Even before Carl's prick was aligned at the pucker of Jack's butt, Jack's hands experimented with the pleasures to be had from receiving coconut "head". From what Jack could initially tell, guiding the hole-punctured nut up to his cockhead, then down to his cockroot, then up again, he was really going to enjoy this. That his enjoyment would be increased even more, once Carl's stiffness was buried to its balls up Jack's behind, was a given.

Speaking of Carl's stiffness, it was getting harder by the second.

Carl was excited. REALLY excited. It had been well over two years since he'd fucked anyone who looked as good as Jack looked, whose ass looked as damned good and as inviting as Jack's ass looked. Hell, maybe, he'd never fucked someone who looked quite this good, whose ass looked quite so inviting.

Carl's hands actually trembled as they pried Jack's luscious ass open along its crack. Beneath Carl's fingertips, Jack's asscheeks dimpled and undimpled as Jack's hard cock poked the depths of Cory Coconut's head, then pulled almost free. At the same time, Jack's asspucker pursed and unpursed, in open invitation for a kiss by the mouth of Carl's readily primed cock.

Despite himself, Carl began to drool. Literally. Great washes of saliva filled his mouth and overflowed. His swallowing and the frantic licks of his tongue weren't sufficient to keep his lips free of slobber. He imagined strings of goo trailing his chin, dripping mucous onto his chest and belly, even painting opaque designs in his pubic hair.

Carl curved his left hand and wedged his fingertips down through Jack's asscrack from the top. By fanning his fingers, he kept open enough space, between Jack's tight assbuns, to target Jack's awaiting pucker that was parenthesized by its halo of accompanying musk-drenched black hair.

Carl's right hand pulled Carl's dick onto the target and threatened to snap off his cock at its base. Then, more than ever, Carl suspected he might have, here, in Jack, too much of a good thing, considering the inferior goods that had come before. Nevertheless, Carl was helpless to slow down his rising passion. He was more and more desperate for the feel of his cock feeding Jack's rectum, his seven inches ass-gobbled to where there would be no available prick left to follow.

Jack wasn't concerned that Carl took so long. He knew the advantages in not rushing a fuck. Anticipation was a powerful aphrodisiac. Not immediately having Carl's dick made Jack want it all the more. Even thinking about that moment, upcoming, when Carl's cock would push totally on through, made the sensations, from Jack fucking the coconut, jump to an even more intense level.

The tight fit of Jack's cock in the coconut, combined with the cocoa butter which acted as sealant as well as lubricant, made a vacuum that became stronger each time an outward stroke of Jack's erection pumped out more of the water and water that sloshed the nut's guts. It was as if the coconut were real head, motivated by real brain that was consciously working to make this a blow-job Jack wouldn't soon forget.

"Ah, yes," Jack greeted the further placement of Carl's rubberized cockhead against Jack's anal doorway. Jack widened his stance for better balance. The last thing he wanted was to be bowled over, literally, by the experience.

Good thing Jack was prepared, because Carl was pretty much already out of control. If he, like Jack, knew the advantages to a long and leisurely screw, it was a more primitive and needy part of his brain that rammed his cock home with such vengeance.

"Ughh!" Jack responded and simultaneously pulled the coconut down securely against his crotch to help maintain his balance.

The men's combined stability was, likewise, aided by how

quickly Carl, his cock pushed deep up Jack's tight butt, took hold of Jack's hips and pulled back.

"Oh, sweet, sweet ass," Carl announced for all the world to hear; although, he hoped only Jack and he were listening. Nor was his opinion of Jack's sweet ass changed when that sweet, growing ever sweeter by the minute, ass exerted internal pressure that seemingly squeezed Carl's dick to half its circumference and extended the same prick to twice its length. The mere sensation of having so much of his cock plugged up this stud's rectum did even more pleasurable things to Carl's guts. Although the fucking had just begun, Carl already had about as much of it as he could take, this first session.

"That's right, fuck me," Jack encouraged and provided another crunch of his asshole around Carl's dick plugged into it. Had he known how far gone Carl was, he might have left out the squeeze. He certainly would have left out the sudden circular movement of his clenched ass that shot Carl through and through with pleasure while it, likewise, threatened to twist Carl's cock off at its base.

"Sorry," was all Carl could say when it became obvious all the fucking he needed, this time, for orgasm, had been the one-way ride of his cock up this stud's butt. "Sorry," he repeated as the passions inside of him reached boiling and wouldn't be denied. "Sorry," he mumbled as the fireworks started, deep in his belly, and flashed outward, from point of origin, like a star in supernova. "Sorry!" he grunted gutturally as his butt-buried cock shot bullet after bullet of thick and coagulated cream into the nippled end of the black condom that ballooned to provide barely adequate containment.

When it had finally dawned on Jack that Carl wasn't, at least this time, going to spend any real length of time riding ass, Jack had proceeded with a quick series of hasty pumps of the coconut over his cock. When he knew he no longer had a reason to delay his orgasm, he turned off all conscious effort to prevent it and went with the flow. His hands piston-pumped the coconut over his cock faster than any real head would have managed, and he achieved his orgasm if not in direct sync with Carl's premature explosion then not all that far behind it. In fact, although cum-spent, Carl's cock was still hard, inside Jack's butt, when Jack's eruption put Carl's already cum-exhausted piece of meat through the additional prick-twisting wringer.

Carl held on for dear life, the exquisite pleasure/pain of his climax-sensitized prick being mauled by Jack's orgasmic anal contractions (caused by Jack's force-feeding cum to the gullet of the coconut), enough to push Carl into another, albeit dry, orgasm.

"Sorry," was all Carl could again manage when he finally found his speaking voice which had temporarily deserted him.

"Sorry for what?" Jack wanted to know. "You got your rocks off. I got my rocks off. You wanted more?"

If Jack would have suggested they begin again, right then and there, Carl would have thrown caution to the wind and taken him up on the offer. He'd later thank God that one of them had kept his wits about him.

"We'll have plenty of time for more fun and games," Jack promised, then reminded: "But, right now, I think you have a Swahili lesson."

"Jesus!" was Carl's exclamation of agreement and disappointment.

CHAPTER 3

Jack stayed on at the museum after Carl left. Doing so fit in with his cover for being on the island.

He sought out Jasper and handed over to the Negro the posted fee of admission. It had been so long since the museum had seen a paying visitor, Jasper looked embarressedly uncertain as to what he was supposed to do with the cash. Certainly, there were no tickets around from better times. Official entry now consisted merely of Jasper ushering Jack back into the main room and leaving him blessedly on his own.

It would have taken no effort at all to break into any cabinet. There were ways, too, to spirit almost anything off the island, other than through official channels. Except, was there really anything in the room worth the effort? Livingstone's papers, water-stained and alga-green, looked as if they'd disintegrate if exposed to any more air or moisture.

Jack lingered over the Livingstone exhibit, with its diary opened on pages whose time-faded ink might detail an expedition's manifest, or, maybe, its laundry list. With its compass (directional designates rusted illegibly), its sextant (did anyone ever use one of those things to find distances anywhere but at sea?), one riding boot (with no explanation as to what had happened to its mate), two moth-eaten cloth gloves (black, now; maybe, once, pearl grey; maybe, once, even, white) ...

If Jack looked, and he did, he really didn't see, because his mind, momentarily, was elsewhere. Focused on how one fucked a coconut to best milk the most pleasure out of it. Or, was the correct terminology "to coconut-milk it"? That play on words made him smile.

Slaves

He bent slightly at his knees to better adjust the inconvenient way his cock was suddenly swelling within his trousers. His fingers still lingered, almost lovingly, over the bulge of his stiff prick, when he realized he wasn't alone in the room. He expected Jasper, surprised when it wasn't.

"Jack Mallard?"

Jack tried not to be too obvious in the way his hand swung free of his crotch to rest atop a nearby display case.

"Do I know you?" Jack's question superfluous, in that, of course, he didn't know this African stud. He would have remembered. Although he preferred his men blond, blue-eyed and beautiful, his tastes, overall, were extremely eclectic. Luckily for him, especially considering the business he was in, he could appreciate a well-put-together male no matter how tall or short, heavy or thin, big-cocked or small, black or white, yellow or red ... or, in this instance, black.

"Konoco Fassal," the newcomer introduced.

"Ah, the man it's been arranged I meet at the tourist bureau, regarding my research paper," Jack realized. "A coincidence you've run across me here?"

"Hardly," Konoco's smile broadened. His sensuously full lips, a light charcoal, revealed a perfect line of dazzling white teeth. "Rather labyrinthine, if you must know the truth. Let's see if I can get it right in the telling." He took a deep breath. "I missed you at the airport, meaning to meet you there, but was told you'd safely arrived and were probably headed to your hotel. I missed you at your hotel but was told you'd left, foolishly without a hat; although no one dared tell you of your silliness, lest someone risk the possibly of offending one of our so-rare-these-days American tourists. Tracking a hatless American on Zanzibar streets not all that difficult. A cousin of mine, actually, the one who told me you'd been rescued by Dr. Mider. Dr. Mider assigned a room here, because of his interest in the local flora, of which this museum has the island's most impressive collection."

With an almost fluid grace, more dancer than tour guide from the local Tanzania Tourist and Friendship Bureau, Konoco moved passed Jack.

"This exhibit, for instance, has proved extremely interesting to Dr. Mider," Konoco said and indicated the tall cabinet beside which he'd taken up position. "Malele: a dried lichen, powdered as a cure for the common headache. Mbarika: its oil a purge, its leaves a binding for strains, its stem juice (when mixed with the leaves of the pigeon pea), a styptic. Etcetera."

Jack obliged by moving in for a closer look. What he found in the same display was the more easily identifiable clove: a spice synonymous with Zanzibar before the revolution had disrupted production and deposed, usually quite fatally, all Arab plantation owners. There was mention of eugenol on the accompanying placard: a clove derivative used in perfumes and flavorings.

"But you seemed more turned on by the Livingstone items." The way Konoco said "turned on" could easily indicate that he'd not missed Jack's fingering of boner-in-trousers, nor the bulge Jack's erection continued to make in Jack's pants.

"Just making my way around the room," Jack excused.

"Speaking of 'making it around' ... our little island, as opposed to our little museum ... I've lined up a few sites that I think you'll find of interest, by way of background material for your paper. No hurry, mind you. I'm merely here, because it ended up convenient to where I was headed. My cousin lives just down the street."

Konoco smiled again. Extraordinary: the way his dazzling white teeth contrasted with the rich blackness of most the rest of him.

"Don't miss the most important pieces of historical

memorabilia, as far as your paper is concerned, hidden though they may be in their own little corner," Konoco said and motioned Jack to a display case at the very end of the far wall. Without any conscious effort, Jack was drawn along in the black man's wake.

"Ah, yes," Jack said, immediately recognizing what he was shown.

"Totems of Zanzibar's eternal shame," Konoco said. Whether his tone was dead-serious, or tinged with the amusement his grin indicated, was hard for Jack to tell. "Rallying signs around which our proletariat eventually arose to eliminate all Arabs and their long-time control of the island. Although, as you probably very well know, by the time the revolt occurred, slavery had been prohibited for years, the Arab control merely a question of land rights."

The display cabinet held a jumble of chains, manacles, yokes, shackles, handcuffs, fetters, stocks and bonds, whips, a whipping post, a ...

"Pillory," Konoco singled out the stained wooden frame with its holes for locking someone's head and hands in place. "The Arab who owned my grandfather, not all that long ago — when Arabs were truly slave masters, and most of us blacks were slaves — put him in one of these on a regular basis. He'd drop my grandaddy's drawers and beat my grandaddy's bare butt with a whip much like that one." He indicated a cat-o'-nine-tails a little less vicious than its metal-studded companion. "Of course, grandfather always boasted, when telling the tale, that he had quite the studly and firm ass, back in those days. I only knew him, you understand, when his butt sagged almost as far toward the floor as some old women's tits."

"Interesting," Jack said. Certainly it was that, even if it wasn't exactly the kind of background material Jack expected from his official greeter.

"After each beating of my grandaddy's ass, the Arab fucked it."

A revelation which Jack found even more surprising. Not that he didn't believe it was true; he just couldn't believe he'd been made privy to such personal family information.

"Happened regularly, for years and years," Konoco continued, "whenever the Arab suspected grandaddy was getting a bit too uppity and needed to be taken down a peg or two. According to grandaddy, the Arab never did learn that my grandfather liked getting his ass whipped and fucked. Personally, I find it interesting that the Arab never sold my grandfather, when other slaves were on and off the island, in those days, quicker than flies landed on and were waved off fresh meat."

Konoco pursed his lips and rolled his eyes thoughtfully.

"I suppose you find that a bit risquÈ," he decided. "Which leads me to suspect that male-male sex, actually so much a part of my island's slave-trade days, is destined, yet again, to be short-changed."

"Maybe you could arrange for me to interview your grandfather," Jack suggested. Actually, Jack, while probably regularly servicing Carl, would be very interested in hearing what the old man had to say about the gay old slave days.

"I'm afraid you'd have to be quite the clairvoyant to speak to grandaddy, these days."

"He's dead," Jack divined.

"At one-hundred-and-two. Happy he was to go, too. He didn't particularly like Zanzibar after the end of slavery. Liked it even less when all the Arabs were murdered and/or expelled. He certainly was never fond of those presently in control. I suspect he missed those ass-whips and butt-fucks given him by his Arab master. I'm even more convinced he missed his ass no longer as firm and studly as it once was."

"I do find all of this extremely interesting." No lie! "But..." Jack overexaggerated his genuine checking out of all sides of the cabinet, underneath it, and around and underneath a nearby table. "... should I be looking for hidden microphones?"

"Ah!" Konoco's accompanying laugh was loud, merry, and seemingly genuine. "Because homosexuality is against our present laws, you mean?"

"I didn't get that part wrong, then?"

"As far as those hidden microphones, I doubt my government has immediate access to even the lowest-level technology. Even if it did, I doubt it would be able to afford it."

That sounded so similar to what Carl had said that Jack could only wonder if his conversation with Carl had been recorded, fed back to him now.

"On the other hand, you shouldn't be too surprised if you end up propositioned by more than one Zanzibar man, boy, girl, or woman, before you leave," Konoco said. "Even in these contemporary times, fucking — butt, cunt, mouth, or whatever — inevitably finds its own way. Especially since we are, at present, a very poor nation, where many of us have nothing of value to sell, except ourselves. That being the case, laws that are, in fact, on our books, are often overlooked, in that jailing every Zanzibar native who sexually fraternized with a tourist would see a sizable portion of our population, male and female, young and old, behind bars. Not to mention see the loss of badly needed foreign currency. Speaking of which, do feel free, on occasion, to part with one or more of your American one-dollar bills. How many did you carry with you through customs? A hundred of them, was it?"

"I had intended to use them as tips but was specifically warned, as was every other passenger on the plane, that giving money, other than local currency obtained through a government-licensed exchange, was entirely prohibited."

"Do you know what an American one-dollar bill buys on Zanzibar these days? A pair of black-market Nike tennis shoes; not old but brand-spanking new. Or, two whole days of sight-seeing, meals, included. Or, pussy galore, if you're so inclined (and, no, that's not a reference to a female protagonist in some James Bond movie). Or, assholes and cocks galore, if you've a yen to go in that direction."

"You left out 'jail time'," Jack reminded. "And no US consulate handy with enough pull to yank whatever strings necessary to get any American offender out of prison."

"We arrest an American tourist, such visitors already so rare on our island, and when do you think the next one is likely to arrive on our shores? Remembering, please, that the government is as anxious for your dollars, and what your dollars can buy, as is the ordinary man on our streets. The warning, given you on the plane as you landed, not to part with your money except to a government-authorized exchange, merely a ruse of the local authorities to put all of your dollars in their pockets, not mine. When did you last hear of our having arrested any tourist, no matter his nationality?"

"I wouldn't want to be the first, in that very long time."

Konoco smiled, then checked his watch.

"I've my cousin waiting," he said. "What say I drop by your hotel tomorrow morning to see what we can do about firming up your itinerary? Maybe even do a bit of sigh-seeing to get you oriented to the possibilities?"

"I'll look forward to it."

Konoco left, and Jack turned back to the cabinet and its items so indicative of Zanzibar's once so-very-important slave trade. Jack imagined what it had been like for that Arab who'd had the unquestionable power to command Konoco's grandfather to drop his pants and offer up neck and wrists for the pillory, to offer up black ass to the skin-blistering strokes of a cat-o'-nine-tails, to offer up the funky depths of black asshole to fucking Arab cock, and have it all happen, without a hitch. Just because the Arab wanted to screw firm and studly Negro butt.

When he got back to his room at the hotel, Jack's thoughts were still of that black man in that pillory. The black man, though, was no longer Konoco's grandfather; it as Konoco. It was no longer an Arab whose power could command black ass; it was Jack.

"Drop your pants, black bastard!" Jack commanded. Except, as he stood there, in front of the cracked and discolored full-length hotel mirror, it was Jack who dropped his pants.

The crotch of his undershorts was bulged with his erection. His cockhead had fucked its way to freedom, beyond the elastic waistband, and his cockhead's knob-like mass, in all its splendor, rested above the cupping of Jack's navel.

"Shuck it all, blacky!" Jack commanded his own image and took off his shirt and undershirt.

The fly of his underpants was soaked with the natural lubricant which had continuously leaked from his cock ever since his boner had begun reformation amid the display cases of the museum. Sticky webbing of goo made itself evident when Jack tugged at the wet-cotton crotch of his underpants to air his total drool-drenched prick and its slimed belly.

"Proud of that big black cock, aren't you, black man?" Jack asked, dropped his shorts and stepped out of them. "But, it's not that big stiff meat of yours that interests me, is it? So, let's see that firm and studly black ass of yours."

He turned his well-formed butt to the mirror. His was a firm ass. His was a studly ass. So what that it was a white and not a black ass? This was fantasy time!

"Maybe, this time, I'll grab that big black prick of yours and whip it for white cream, even while I fuck the shit out of your cat-o'-nine-tails whipped black ass with my lily-white dick," Jack said. "Would you like that?"

No pillory in the hotel room, but Jack imagined Konoco secured in one. If Jack laid on the hotel bed, the mildew on the bedspread clammy beneath his butt and back, he was, in his mind, standing behind Konoco, his cock ready for the hot plunge up restrained Negro's funky ass.

His left hand pulled his cock to launch position. His right hand fisted and topped the head of his boner.

"My cock is at your door, black man," Jack said and shut his eyes. "I'm going to fuck my pale cock up your inky asshole, and there's nothing whatsoever you can do about it. Nothing." His fist opened under the pressure of its lowering over his dick. His grip slid along his prick to where the heel of his fist crunched the black hair haloing the base of his erection. He gave several tight and fast pumps.

"Fuck that tight black ass," he said.

He moved into a slower, more methodical, masturbatory rhythm.

"We're getting into the swing of things, now, aren't we, slave stud?" he said.

His fist provided an accompanying little twist that increased friction and pleasure.

"Yes, yes," he complimented his own expertise. He'd had enough practice, beating his meat, to have mastered all the tricks of doing it the best way. He knew just how firm to make his grip. Just how far, up and down, to slide, on each and every pump. Just how hard and how fast to move his fist, over his dick, in order to connect to each and every hint of pleasure.

The disadvantage of whipping his own meat was that he was so familiar with what best pleased him that it made for a fast progression from start to finish. Which was okay if he was

Slaves

out for a quick blasting to relieve a bit of stress or tension.
However, when he was into a really good fantasy-fuck, like butt-
plugging a pillory-locked Negro slave, and when he wanted to
make that fantasy last, it required his trading off some of the
pleasures of a mechanically perfect jerk-off for the pleasures of
a fantasy made longer-lasting by a bit of well-planned
masturbatory ineptitude.

"We're going to make this last, Konoco, my man, because
you've been a really bad slave, haven't you?"

Jack continued on his merry way. His eyes shut, the
imagery of Konoco, head and hands locked up, ass jutting out
for fucking, Jack's cock inside that charcoal puckered butt, was
all played out, in living black and white, across the back of
Jack's closed lids.

If he tried really hard, Jack could hear the sexy slap, slap,
slap of his belly as it rammed Konoco's ass, on each and every
inward swing. If he listened really carefully, he could hear
Konoco's groans of pleasure/pain as Jack's big cock raped the
black man's asshole.

Suddenly, Jack realized it wasn't Konoco groaning but Jack
who was making all the guttural noise.

His free hand ran up his belly to his chest. It found one of
his nipples, already tack-hard, and tweaked it to additional
tautness.

"Tell me, Konoco, how do you like getting your upstanding,
charcoal nipple tugged even harder?" he demanded. Then, he
followed up with, "I like it fine when you do it, Massah. I like it
real fine."

Jack found and pinched his other nipple, ever harder.

"How about that, Konoco?" he asked his phantom lover.
Then answered, "Good boss. I mean, real good. No one
pinches this black man's pap better than white Massah Mallard
does."

Jack kept on until his pain was more obvious but hadn't yet overridden his pleasure. He wanted ache and enjoyment in perfect harmony, and he got it.

He left off tweaking his nipples and dropped his hand down his chest and belly. He flattened his palm, his fingers splayed and aimed toward his crotch. He wedged the thick root of his cock in between the fuckfinger and ring finger of his hand. He pressed down and squeezed inward around the submerged anchoring of his cock inside his belly. His erection stood higher and stiffer.

"Oh ... what ... a good ... black ... slave ... fuck ... you ... are," he congratulated his game-playing. His pleasure swelled at just the right momentum for him to enjoy fully the scenario his mind's-eye continued so successfully to play out for him.

A few more pumps of his hand, over his stiff meat, combined with a few more imaginings of Konoco's black ass, swallowing the thick white inches of Jack's dick, and Jack would have one helluva geyser in his hand.

Before his climax, he withdrew his pinching fingers from his cockroot, and he slid that entire hand, around his left thigh, all of the way to where he could pinch his left asscheek. He bent his knees and placed his feet flat on the bedspread. All the while beating his cock, he guided his left hand's fuckfinger to his damp asspucker.

At that precise moment, Jack's fantasy changed from his being the one who fucked to his being the one getting fucked.

No longer was it Konoco anchored securely within the pillory; it was a naked and vulnerable Jack there. No longer was it Konoco's black ass fucked by Jack's white cock; it was Jack's white ass poked and re-poked by Zanzibar Negro's thick, black truncheon. It was no longer Konoco responding to the verbal commands of his white master; it was Jack begging ... "Fuck me, fuck me, Jesus, fuck me!" ... as Jack's fuckfinger unceremoniously dug faster and deeper up his white man's butt.

Jack's hips lifted his asshole even more securely over his raping finger.

"Oh, black Massah!" he grunted, and his violated asswalls hugged his intruding finger like super glue might grip wooden dowel. His cock went harder and even more drooly in his pumping fist.

It wasn't long to blast-off. No denying it. If imagining himself raping Negro ass had been a turn-on, even Jack was surprised by how much more exciting the idea of himself on the receiving end of raping black cock.

"Oh, black Massah, I'm going to cum," he said.

He crooked his fuckfinger where it was screwed up his butt. His submerged fingertip found and jabbed his prostate, then jabbed it again, and screwed hard against it.

Jack performed an abdominal "crunch", the likes of which physical-fitness instructors always insist is better for flattening a belly than any old-fashioned sit-up ever could be. Jack's suddenly opened eyes had full view of his trembling hunk of thick meat as it continued to be strangled by his hand. His chest and stomach muscles were thrust into high relief and provided an attractively scalloped and narrow valley that ran from the base of his neck to his belly button. His navel was compressed into no more than a winked eye.

His cock blew, right then and there. Creamy magma erupted from the golden upthrust of his gloriously volcanic male meat. His cum spewed in rapid pulses that hurled great gobs so far that the first of them stuck to Jack's partially opened mouth; he licked at their salty deliciousness. The next bursts splattered his chest and his belly. The last of his cream, unsuccessful in exiting his cock but still stuffing his meaty cockshaft, like whipped cream stuffing a white-pastry eclair, got squeezed to freedom by the final, jerky compression of Jack's still-hugging hand.

Frosting-like white drool oozed out and over his orgasm-reddened cockhead, filled the ridge Jack's upper fist made around his cockneck. Then, even more tardy slime added to the cum-flow, and Jack's fingers became webbed with the same goo that soon formed opaque streamers amid that black pubic hair awaiting in the hairy cushion at Jack's fist-battered crotch.

CHAPTER 4

Jack asked for Scotch. No ice. No water. No way did he trust the bottled water on Zanzibar without personally seeing the seal being broken. Maybe not even then. Certainly he trusted none of the rust-laden and probably bacteria-laden water that gushed from the antiquated hotel plumbing system.

Someone called out to Jack and asked if he was American.

Jack turned to the corner table occupied by Field Speer and an unidentified young man.

Field was overweight in a safari outfit that seemed at least a size too small. Two jacket buttons, fastened at his belly, but only barely, showed all indications of about-to-pop. A suitably sized oversized T-shirt kept his pale belly flesh from spilling into view.

Pale was the overall impression given by Field. Particularly noticeable on a tropical island where everyone else was one degree or another of tan to black.

Even his hair, once blond, was now pale as ash.

When Jack got close enough to see Field's eyes, almost lost within facial features that merged overhanging eyebrows and plump cheeks with two distinct layers of jowls, he half expected, despite already knowing otherwise, that Field's eyes would be albino pink. Actually, Field's eyes were attractive grey. What's more, they possessed an inherent intelligence that would have been as surprising as unexpected had Jack not known Field responsible for the whole project in which Jack was presently involved.

"I thought I was the lone Yank on this godforsaken dot in the middle of nowhere," Field lied convincingly and waved Jack into the chair across from him. "Thought for a brief moment that

Slaves

Ferdinand, here, was American, his English so damned good, but turns out he's from the Philippines."

"Ferdinand Makin," self-introduced the boyish young man on Field's immediate right. He extended his hand and gripped Jack's responsive fingers in a briefly firm but not bone-crushing squeeze.

Ferdinand's hair was a crisp jet-black, short and feather-cut to keep its usually straight strands in place. The styling didn't quite succeed, because his hair slightly, albeit attractively, banged his forehead.

His black eyes weren't in the least slanted, wide-spaced, one on either side of his delicate nose. His mouth possessed brown, full-blown lips. His skin was pleasantly bronze.

His body looked tightly compact within his blue-linen suit. He wore a blue tie, same shade blue as his suit, and its purposely loose knot was fashionably drooped below the unbuttoned top button of his white cotton shirt to reveal an attractive vee of perfectly hairless chest.

"Jack Mallard," Jack introduced himself.

"Like the duck," Field said.

"Like the portable mechanism for lifting heavy objects a short distance."

"What? Oh, 'jack', you mean," Field said and laughed appreciatively. "Well, Jack/jack, I'm here to talk to the government about possibly buying some cloves. Ferdinand is here to photograph the island monkeys, as if the world isn't full of monkeys these days. And you're here to ...?"

"Do a paper on the once-flourishing slave trade."

"Speaking of photographing monkeys," Ferdinand said and got to his feet, "I've film that needs developing before tomorrow's outgoing."

"That can wait," Field insisted. "I'm buying the next round, you know?" he said loud enough for the bartender to understand Field had placed an order.

"Thanks, but ..." Ferdinand waved to get the bartender's attention. "... not for me, please." Directly to Field: "A rain check?" To Jack: "Nice to have met you."

Jack and Field watched Ferdinand exit.

The bartender, a studly young black with short-cropped kinky black hair and expressive black eyes, brought two refills and returned to his position behind the bar.

"Watch that one," Field said. "He's one of the competition's minions."

"The bartender?"

Field laughed. Loud. Robust. He smelled vaguely of talcum and cloves.

"Ferdinand Makin," Field said. "On me like a vampire on blood. You find him attractive?"

Jack shrugged.

"Didn't mean to be intrusive, dear boy," Field said. "I would have asked the same question had you been straight-as-a-stick and Ferdinand an attractive young woman. Because I've never had a clue as regards what a man does and doesn't find sexy in a man or a woman."

Jack wasn't sure he believed it, but it was the prevailing rumor.

"True!" Field sensed Jack's doubts. "Cross my heart." He did just that. "People tell me I'm well out of the sexual whirlpool, missing absolutely nothing but heartache and the prospect of catching some death-dealing disease. Sometimes, though, I can't help but wonder what-if-?"

"Want me to see if I can bed Mr. Makin for some pillow talk?" Jack wasn't being sarcastic.

"Not unless he begins to fly a little too far and wide from where I can sufficiently keep an eye on him," Field said. "You and Carl meet up okay?"

"Also, met my liaison with the tourist bureau. Know anything about Konoco Fassal?"

"I'll find out something. Until I do, assume he's directly associated with the police, the government, or both."

"I'm meeting him tomorrow to see some sights and hammer out my itinerary."

Field drained his glass and pushed himself to his feet.

"We must do this again soon," he said. "We Yanks have to stick together. Maybe supper, but not tonight. My tummy's been acting up. Don't get up. Finish your drink. Shall I buy you another?"

"This'll do nicely, thanks."

"I do hope you enjoy your stay on Zanzibar, young man," Field said, expansively, "but were I your age, and if I looked anything like you, I wouldn't be spending my time on this long-dead island, writing some boring paper on a long-dead slave trade."

Jack finished his drink, went to his room, plopped on a bed that exuded, as it had from Jack's arrival, unpleasant odors of mold and mildew.

The room was as hot as it was muggy.

There was a ceiling fan, but it didn't work. There was a huge and ugly air-conditioning unit that didn't work. There were widows, as well as French doors, that opened onto a small balcony, none of which, because of the constant heat, humidity, and neglect, could be pried open, as securely fixed in place as if by lock and key.

Languidly Jack undid his trouser crotch and fisted his dick through the breached material and through the pee-slit provided by his briefs. Something about the climate made his soft dick seem even more impressively large and bulky than usual.

He played his cock to erection but lost interest. He shut his eyes but didn't figure, for a moment, he'd be able to sleep in such a sauna-like atmosphere.

Two hours later, he awoke to his soft dick and darkness. He pushed his prick into his pants, got off the bed too fast and spent the next three seconds trying to rid himself of dizziness.

His hair was damp with sweat, his skin soaked with it, his clothes stained with it.

He found his way to the bathroom, clicking light switches as he went. Not that many lights came on. A total of two, out of the available six in the bedroom, managed any luminescence at all. Closer examination revealed two of the bedroom lamps didn't even have bulbs. Only one light lit the bathroom from a wide assortment of dead bulbs and empty sockets.

Jack ran water in the he sink, thinking to splash his face with refreshing coolness. His hands actually cupped a pool of tepid issue from the faucet when he realized the water was orange. He dumped the hand-reservoired contents into the cracked porcelain of the washbowl and let more water run with the hope of seeing pipes, some time soon, cleanse themselves of whatever their iron-based encrustations. He leaned against the sink and took a good look at himself as reflected from the mirror.

Although he felt hot, confined, and put-upon by the lack of amenities, he looked damned good. His hair was of the right thickness and length to appear stylishly well-ordered, even when wet, even when the wet was an overflow of scalp sweat. Perspiration glossed his tanned skin to burnished gold. Even the poor lighting added an attractive quality to his reflection, like the inherent shadowing of a Rembrandt oil.

He turned off the faucet, which still ran rust, and decided on a bath, after first checking his watch to be sure he would, if late, not be so late as to miss the last-serve deadline in the dining room. Although, he hated to imagine what culinary concoctions brewed by the kitchen staff.

Slaves

The bathtub plumbing proved no less cooperative than that of the sink. It provided a long-lasting cacophony of sound — grunts, gurgles, clangs, bangs, whistles, hoots — before any water deigned appear. When the liquid finally flowed, with spasmodic coughs reminiscent of a TB victim, it came compete with seemingly blood-tainted spume.

After five minutes, Jack realized the water was never going to clear completely, so he plugged the drain with the gunk-stained stopper, and let the metal-tainted fluid rise over rings etched in the bathtub as obviously as any receding lake's shoreline ever etched sandstone.

Only because he was hot and sweaty did he risk the resulting discolored pool that was as tempting as a primordial swamp. When he slipped his ass down the slideway of porcelain, opposite the faucet, and surrendered his body to the tea-like solution, the water was sufficiently dark to hide all trace of his cock, balls, legs, and feet.

Immediately, his cock and scrotum responded to their dousing by constricting in protest. Jack actually felt his scrotal sac lose as much slack as it sometimes did during orgasm, bringing his balls up high against the base of his dick. His cock might as well have been dunked in ice water, the way it deflated from its usual state of limp impressiveness.

He completed his bath in record time, the water not as cold as he would have liked it, but wet nonetheless. He even washed his hair, although he could only imagine what the long-time effects would be. His only consolation was that Zanzibari had to be subjected to much the same phenomenon, on a daily basis, and none, at least as seen by him so far, seemed to suffer any visible consequences.

When he arose from the water, his genitalia were as small as he'd ever seen. So small, he immediately played with his cock until entirely reassured that its newly shrunken condition was only temporary and not a permanent emasculation rendered by the unsavory liquid.

He dried, dressed, wrestled open the door to the hallway and found his way to an almost deserted dining room. There were only two other diners, both middle-aged men, one with a monocle (the first Jack had ever seen actually used), the second with a baggy brown suit which might have been comfortable but did nothing for the man's already dumpy physique. Both men were secluded little islands, separated by a sea of empty tables and chairs. Jack was seated so as to form his own separate island, so far removed from the others that there was not the least chance of easy conversation.

The evening meal, no options offered, was South African lobster. Which seemed a tad luxurious only for as long as it took to realize South Africa wasn't all that far away. In fact, if one wanted to argue the point, Zanzibar was south Africa, being below the Equator.

The lobster tasted particularly bland, even if Jack always found all lobster bland, and it came across particularly chewy. The accompanying rice pilaff was barely warm, whether because it was from the bottom of the pot, or because it had never been hot in the first place. The dinner rolls were hard as rocks and just as difficult to open as geodes. Once open, their interiors were stale and vaguely grey.

Jack drank warm beer, after first inspecting the bottle to be sure the original cap was sealed in place and dislodged at-table.

When he left the room, the other two men were still there. The monocled gentleman read a Swedish paperback novel, the baggy-suited gentleman examined papers apparently fetched from the open briefcase at one side of his chair.

Jack's original thoughts were to return to his oppressive room, but he detoured in favor of forced exit through a humidity-warped side door that gave access to the fecundity of a once-formal garden run riot. The existing vegetation was a veritable tangle and maze of high-growing trees, strangling and strangled vines, huge bushes, and night-blooming flowers. The latter oozed a slightly too cloyingly sweet perfume to the still-hot and steamy evening air. Jack only knew he confronted a garden, not a jungle, because of crumbling masonry that once apparently confined what was now in such obvious overflow.

Straight above, the panoply of star-studded black night sky, exotic in its display of constellations unseen in the northern hemisphere, was made all the more dazzling by so little competition from ground light. If there was a moon, Jack didn't see it. He didn't see the ocean, either, but only heard its water in constant flux. He headed in the direction of the water. Not directly into the garden overgrowth, because that route seemed quickly to dead-end among trunks and vines, but into a narrow runway between the vegetation's leading edge and the hotel.

The beauty of the ocean, extended to an island-dotted horizon, the shadowy silhouette of a distant freighter, the shimmering cascade of suddenly visible moon reflected off the water, the expanse of startling white beach, was really quite marvellous at the end of the claustrophobic passageway Jack took to get there.

The breeze off the water was downright refreshing and managed to blow away just enough of the night-flower perfume to make the residue fragrance actually pleasant.

The sound of another warped hotel door being forced open caused Jack reflexively to step back into the shadows from which he'd just exited.

Although he couldn't see who, he heard the distinctive sounds of someone stepped onto the verandah that provided the hotel its porch as far as the beach.

Jack stayed where he was, because he didn't want to make

small-talk. He had his cover story down pat, but sometimes needing to keep every woof and weave of that convoluted tapestry straight was more bother than it was worth.

The appearance of Ferdinand Makin, however, leaving the leading lip of the porch and strolling the sand immediately in front of Jack, got Jack's attention. Jack's first reaction was that the Filipino had followed Jack, Ferdinand somehow made suspicious by Jack's meeting up with Field Speer in the hotel bar. Ferdinand now out to keep an eye on what Jack might really be up to. Except, Ferdinand wasn't likely to have guessed which route Jack would take, once Jack had exited the side door. Even Jack hadn't known that he'd turn toward the ocean until the very second he'd done so. Nor had Ferdinand been all that undercover when he'd bullied open the door and now walked the beach in full view.

So, Jack milked his unexpected opportunity to keep an eye on Ferdinand's activities within the encompassing Zanzibar night. Keeping the shadowy backdrop of the garden-jungle to his left, Jack paralleled Ferdinand's continuing meander through the sand.

The young Filipino wore a pair of sandals; white pants; a white formal/informal shirt, shirttail out, embroidered in front, like shirts Jack more associated with Mexico than with the Philippines. Probably because Jack had travelled extensively in Mexico but had yet to visit the Philippines where such shirts were an important part of any Filipino man's wardrobe.

So caught up was Jack in shadowing Ferdinand, he not only missed the presence of the Negro kid in the jungle shadows just ahead but would likely have collided with him if the kid, apparently as intent upon Ferdinand as Jack was, hadn't stepped out of concealment and headed onto the beach before Jack reached him.

Jack's heart-in-throat surprise at the kid's sudden

appearance brought Jack up short and stepped him more securely into the greenery. From where Jack watched, the kid's projected course and that of Ferdinand seemed destined to intersect.

Jack tried to memorize the newcomer's features. It was a bit of possibly useful information for Field as regarded the competition's connections with the locals.

Unfortunately, the kid walked on a leftward diagonal that provided Jack with mainly a rear view. It was a nice view, nonetheless, purely from the standpoint of aesthetics, but Field would hardly appreciate, "Really nice ass. I could tell by the way it filled the seat of his cut-offs. Nice legs and back, too. I could tell because he wore shorts and no shirt. Not the back musculature of an adult male but ..."

Ferdinand sensed he was about to be joined and stopped, causing the kid to vary his intended route and swerve into a more direct one.

Jack couldn't hear what was said. Once again, he was pretty well burrowed into the convenient backdrop of vegetation, wanting to see but not be seen.

When Ferdinand and the kid turned in Jack's direction, and headed in what seemed a beeline course right toward him, Jack figured they had him spotted for sure.

Did he stay down, wait for them to walk right up and say to him, "Well, look what we have here!"? Did he stand up, stumble out, mumble some inane nonsense, like, "Thank God! I thought for sure I'd wander around, lost in that nightmare jungle, until hell froze over!"? He still tried to decide when he detected what he thought, hoped, just might be a slight difference in where they were headed, as opposed to where he guiltily awaited their arrival.

Jack suppressed an audible sigh of relief when they entered the bank of vegetation immediately to his left, without a sideways glance in his direction. For just a moment, Jack was so sure that they'd passed right on through, possibly en route to an exit from the garden-jungle on its other side, he was surprised no end when ...

"Money, please, man," someone said, so close that Jack thought whomever it was addressed him. Maybe asking for hush money to keep silent about Jack's little exercise in playing Peeping Tom.

"Half the money," someone else said, and Jack thought he'd heard enough of Ferdinand's speech, brief as it had been, to recognize it here and now.

Suddenly, the black kid seemed more likely to have asked Ferdinand for some kind of pay-off. Would his information, bought and paid for by Ferdinand, be of interest to Field who, via Jack, would get the same information for free?

"All the money up front, man," the kid said.

Jack dared a bit of minimum shifting that better turned him in their direction. At first, he saw nothing but shadow-blackened greenery. Then, quite miraculously, after only a slight tilt of his head to the right, from where he squatted, he accessed a breach of shrubbery that showed him the kid and Ferdinand, less than six feet away. What's more, either Jack's eyes had grown more accustomed to the night, or the moonlight had gotten brighter, because Jack saw surprisingly well, if in varying shades of black, grey and white.

"Half now," Ferdinand said and counted off a few bills from a wad he retrieved from one pocket. He handed over the cash. "The rest after."

The black kid looked young. If not young enough to be verifiable chicken, at least not all that long from the henhouse. He had a short-cropped skullcap of kinky black curls. He had large, wide-set eyes, a thin nose, thick lips, all part of an ebony face that if not exactly handsome, to Jack's way of thinking, certainly didn't have to be bagged to keep the horses from stampeding.

For his age, or seemingly young age, the kid had a surprisingly well-developed chest. Not bulked up, but with muscle groups readily defined. Pectorals, obviously square. Abdominals, obviously washboarded.

The kid took the offered cash and stuffed it deep into the right front pocket of his cut-offs, calling Jack's attention to the kid's basket which was definitely another well-defined muscle, this one ill-concealed by the material tenting his crotch.

"Okay, the rest afterwards," the kid said. His somewhat nervous smile revealed a row of startlingly white teeth.

From Jack's standpoint, the tone of the meeting took an entirely different turn when Ferdinand, after having pocketed his remaining wad of bills, unzipped the fly of his white slacks. Jack was still a bit disoriented when Ferdinand's hand passed in through the breached material and the Filipino's six-inch dick, as well as his accompanying black-furred balls, were hoisted on out into the night air.

Whether such homosexual goings-on were against Zanzibar laws, and they were, the black kid had enough experience to know his cue to drop to his knees.

"Wait one goddamned minute!" Ferdinand said and actually slapped away the kid's hand which had made a grab for Ferdinand's naked dick. "I want my cock rubberized before your mouth is anywhere near it."

"Hey, man, that's not necessary," the kid said. Which Jack found, especially as regarded the projected origins of the AIDS virus, downright scary.

"Hey, man, it is necessary," Ferdinand said; Jack pleased the competition at least had sense enough to recognize the advantages of safe sex. "And, lucky for us both, I just happen to have a rubber handy."

"Let me roll it down your dick," the kid said.

"Let me roll it down my own dick," Ferdinand said. Obviously, he preferred the reassurance of his own safe rubberization of his dick, rather than count upon the efforts of someone who had just suggested the jettisoning of any such precaution.

Ferdinand ripped off the leading edge of a condom packet, squeezed out the rubber, pinched the rubber nipple, and transferred the little latex hat to the head of his now fully erect dick.

Jack found Ferdinand's dick pleasing enough to look at, if not all that bulky or lengthy. Ferdinand's circumcision had been almost flawless, having left only a narrow bridge of scar tissue that connected the belly of the cockhead with the belly of the cockshaft. Aside from that, the penis was pretty straightforward, no bends, no sharp angles, no veins or discolorations or moles distinguishable in the dim lighting.

"What say, I jack-off my own pecker while I eat yours?" the black kid suggested.

"I pay you, you mean, to get your off your own rocks?" Ferdinand added a different perspective.

"What's the harm, man?" the kid insisted. "My hand on my meat always gets me hot and makes me all the hungrier for whatever dick I swing on."

Jack focused all of his ESP toward transmitting to Ferdinand the wherewithal to give the sexy black kid permission. Jack wanted to see the black's cock and match the reality to the impressive expectations held out by the attractive packaging presented by the kid's still concealed crotch.

"I don't want any of your cum on me, got that?" Ferdinand gave explicit instructions. "Keep it contained in your hand, or shoot it in the bushes. I find even a smear of it on me, and there's going to be hell to pay." He made it sound as if he not only could carry through on his warning but that the prophesized consequences would likely be far more dire than the kid could even begin to imagine.

"No problem, man," the kid said and unfastened the fly of his cut-offs.

Jack had never before heard anyone use the term "man" as much as the black kid did, anywhere that is outside of a pretentious movie Jack had once seen about L.A. street gangs.

"See how hard you make my dick, man," the kid said, his cock out of his trousers and in his hand. So quickly out, and followed so equally as fast by the cascade of the kid's hairy balls, it was obvious the kid didn't wear underwear.

Jack had seen bigger cocks and more impressive balls, but none of what the kid offered, even for a price, was anything to toss out of bed.

"Just remember that it's my hard dick that's important here," Ferdinand said. "And while you're remembering that, kindly remember that I don't expect this to take all damned night. Your friend of the other evening ... What was his name? Conrad, was it?"

"Yeah, Conrad, man. Conrad who sure did like sucking your big sweat dick."

Jack thought the "big" a bit of unbridled flattery, considering the contrary evidence at hand, but Ferdinand let it pass without sarcastic comment, possibly more susceptible to flattery than he'd care to admit.

"Well, let's hope Conrad was right when he said you knew a bit more about cocksucking than he does."

"I know lots more about cocksucking than he does, man," the kid said. "I know lots more than most any cocksucker on this island knows. Hell, I taught most of them all they know about sucking dick. 'Cause they and their families are damned hard up unless ...

"Spare me the we-only-suck-dick-for-the-money sad tales," Ferdinand interrupted. "I'm not into the why of it, only the how it feels when I'm on the receiving end."

"Sure, man," the kid said and reached for Ferdinand's cock. This time, Ferdinand let him have at it.

"Conrad said your name was Bongo?" Ferdinand said.

"Bonjo, man," the black corrected. "A name you don't so easily forget once you see the good time Bonjo gives that pretty dick of yours."

"Let's not keep my cock waiting, Bonjo? I wouldn't want a local cop strolling on up and wondering what you, me, and our dicks are up to."

"Local cop would only send me on my merry way and go down on your cock himself, only for a bit more money," Bonjo said and, without farther pause, opened his mouth around the head of Ferdinand's cock and dipped his nose all of the way down and into the open crotch of Ferdinand's cock-sprouting pants.

Although Konoco Fassal, as well as Bonjo, had insinuated the cops weren't all that stringent in enforcing their anti-gay laws, Jack was no more anxious to be discovered where he was than Ferdinand was anxious to be found flagrante delicto. In that Jack would not only have to explain his presence to the authorities but to Ferdinand and Bonjo.

Whatever the chances of discovery by the local cops, however, or by Ferdinand or Bonjo, Jack was definitely stuck where he was for the duration. No way could he risk heading on out, this way or that, without making some noise. A noise which might be mistaken for some foraging animal, but would more likely be easily recognizable as Jack Mallard's ass scuttling through the underbrush.

Besides which, despite the rather inconvenient squat he was in, the show in progress was likely to be well worth whatever his momentary discomfort. It being obvious from the first few bounces of Bonjo's mouth over Ferdinand's cock that the black kid was just as expert at sucking dick as he'd purported to be. Likewise, Bonjo knew more than a little about pleasuring his own cock in the process.

Bonjo's erect penis was more than a handful of black, thick meat, with enough foreskin in reserve, when yanked upward by the kid's own hand, to cowl completely, then literally nipple, the kid's impressively large and charcoal cockcorona.

Jack's viewing pleasure was distorted only by the way his own cock took to swelling in his pants in such a way that didn't allow it to uncoil completely. He did his best to reposition it, first by merely shifting his squat, then by bringing his right hand into play. None of it to any avail.

Finally, he risked the possible noise and dropped to his knees, simultaneously grabbing his pants crotch and manhandling his dick into a more comfortable position inside his trousers. All the while, he kept an eye focused on what Ferdinand and Bonjo were doing, seemingly so close to Jack that Jack felt he had only to reach out in order to cup the Filipino's nuts or seize the black man's sizable balls.

Jack was frustrated as hell that, even after he'd unzipped his pants, he couldn't get his dick and balls into the fresh air as quickly as he wanted. His hard cock had gotten hung up within the piss-passageway provided by the crotch of his briefs.

"Yes, this is a definite improvement over your cock-sucking buddy," Ferdinand admitted, Jack delighted that Ferdinand's speech masked whatever remaining sounds Jack required to get his rebellious dick unfettered.

"Mmmmmm," Bonjo said, his mouth pulled so far up Ferdinand's dick that the black boy's lips actually popped off. "Mmmmmm! Good cock! Delicious meat." Then, anchored to the Filipino's cock once again, he was suddenly all of the way down to Ferdinand's balls.

Jack, his hard prick finally, infinitely more comfortable, now out of his pants and in hand, had trouble deciding whether to concentrate on Bonjo's lips masturbating Ferdinand's dick, or on Bonjo's hand whipping Bonjo's black met. The black man's pumping took on a decidedly sexy torque, in accompaniment to each up and down movement. His black balls rolled within his black scrotum, churning with a life all their own.

"All right!" Ferdinand said, obviously getting into the sensations arising from his sucked cock and sunbursting the rest of his body. "That's just ... how ... I ... like ... it. Yes, yes, yes!"

Ferdinand let Bonjo proceed at his own pace for a short while, then decided to take just a bit more control. He placed his hands over the Negro's ears, took hold of them, like he'd take hold of the handles of a jug, and exerted the pressure necessary to indicate just how he wanted Bonjo to proceed to give Ferdinand his monies' worth.

"You're right that you've a mouth genuinely skillful at cocksucking, and I think I'd really like to take some extra time to enjoy it."

Bonjo had his left hand anchored at the back of Ferdinand's right knee. His right hand, though, continued to pump black dick. Jack noticed that when Ferdinand exerted the pressure that moved Bonjo into a new sucking rhythm, the cadence of Bonjo's fist over Bonjo's black cock changed its rhythm, too.

It was Jack's hand over his own cock that moved fastest. While he knew how enjoyable it might be to attempt to coordinate his rocks off at one and the same time as Ferdinand or Bonjo, Jack didn't want to risk either Ferdinand or Bonjo creaming while Jack still beat his pud. Once one of them creamed, that one's attention would be less self-centred and more apt to hear any of Jack's follow-strokes to climax.

Slaves

Not that Jack's hasty ongoing pumps to pleasure were
accomplished in complete silence. From time to time, he just
couldn't help the little grunts that escaped him. After all,
whipping his meat was pleasurable, in its own right, and the
additional visuals of Bonjo beating his dick senseless, while the
black boy's mouth swallowed and unswallowed the Filipino's
stiff pecker, were enough to make any hand-over-dick voyeur
give an occasional sound or sigh. Luckily, though, the Negro
kid and the Filipino were too involved in their own wet sounds,
and in their own efforts to get it just right, to be all that
completely tuned in to what was going on around them. It
wasn't, after all, as if Jack grunted up a storm. Mostly, his
sounds were as gentle as the sea breeze through the
surrounding jungle-garden leaves and could well be mistaken
for it. Were he any louder, either Bonjo or Ferdinand obviously
would have heard him, even through their building pleasure.
Just as, even up to their climax, they'd undoubtedly hear the
approach of someone along the beach or through the trees.

"Yes, that's the way to do it," Ferdinand said. He made the
most camouflaging noises to leave Jack's comparatively little
sighs undetected. "That is the way to eat my dick. All of the
way from my cockhead ... all of the way to my cockroots. Just
like you are doing now. Just as I want you to keep on doing
until I cream my load ... and fill my condom ... and clog your
throat with cum-ballooned latex."

Bonjo's two nuts, like coconuts minus their outer fiber
husks, although enclosed in a mutual shell more black than
brown, were hugged by scrotum and hoisted to the base of the
black boy's dick, as if one of the local palm trees, and
accompanying fruit, had grown upside-down. Each downward
slide of Bonjo's large hand along the length of his black dick
smashed the heel of his fist against his nuts and made his
testicles even more spheroid.

Alex Von Mann

"Oh, there is just something about fucking my dick up hungry black face that really turns me on," Ferdinand said. "Something about your face, in particular, turns me on, Bonjo. Where your predecessor, Conrad, over my cock, couldn't suck dick for shit and wouldn't have gotten full price-paid for his inept job if he hadn't assured me he had you and your luscious mouth and throat hidden in the wings."

"Mmmmm!" Bonjo said, his face once again on a down-slide that eventually pushed his nose all of the way into the open fly of the Filipino's trousers. There to nestle within the relatively straight strands of pubic hair that grew the base of the bronze-skinned young man's stiffy penis. At one and the same time, Bonjo's chin tucked itself into the pillow offered by Ferdinand's contracted scrotum.

"Maybe with your experienced mouth, it wouldn't be so bad to have this last all night," Ferdinand said and used his handholds on Bonjo's ears to slow the suck down. "Because there's plenty of enjoyment in your sucking my cock, black boy. I can't even remember when I last had my dick sucked with such cock-sucking precision. How many pricks, I wonder, have you feasted on to get you this ... oh, yes, just like that ... good at what you do?"

Maybe Bonjo had sucked enough cocks to know something about Ferdinand's progressed state of arousal, that Jack couldn't tell just by looking, because the black boy's hand began a faster cadence over black dick than Bonjo's face maintained over Ferdinand's pecker. Bonjo, whether correctly or not was yet to be seen, obviously calculated Ferdinand's nuts were destined to blast with less stimulation than was required by Bonjo's fist-encapsulated dick.

Jack was still unprepared to wait for either black or bronze dick to explode before his did, so he made his hand-over-cock cadence even faster than the hand-over-cock and the mouth-over-cock cadences that were presented for his viewing pleasure. He bit his lips to keep from squealing.

Jack had fucked and sucked and jerked off in enough places, many of them surprisingly public, to be confident, then, as now, that he could manage a spurting of cream that wasn't going to call attention to his being where he was. Granted, it took a good deal of control and effort, but Jack had a good deal of control and was willing to make the effort. That was why he was so good at what he did.

"Ugh! Ugh! Ugh!" Ferdinand said, as part of his steadily increasing cacophony of grunts and groans, purrs and mewls, gasps and sighs.

Jack was sure he could come up with a fairly noiseless come, but he was even more confident as Ferdinand began nonstop vocalization.

"Oh, not long. Not long at all," Ferdinand said and let his hips take up a decided fucking motion that pushed his cock forward, each and every time Bonjo's face was on its way down cock, that pulled his cock back, each and every time Bonjo's face was on its slide back up to where only the knob of Ferdinand's dick was socked up the provided hole. "I feel ... my cum ... getting ready ... getting ready ... oh, yes ... getting ready ... to cream."

Bonjo's hand-whipping of his own black cock proceeded into a faster rhythm that would have matched the tempo of Jack's hand over Jack's cock if Jack hadn't, by that time, proceeded on into an even heartier whack of his stiff prick.

Jack was almost ready to let go but not quite. To provide his balls with the extra bit of needed incentive to part with their pearly load, he cupped them and squeezed. Where too much pressure would have provided pain to dampen the rise of Jack's pleasure, the last thing Jack wanted, just enough pain was a supplement to pleasure, which was just what Jack had in mind.

"Yes, yes, yes! I'm about to blow!" Ferdinand said loud enough to put birds to wing.

Except, the garden-jungle, and the whole of Zanzibar, had few birds, most grabbed ages ago for cooking pots. Even Ferdinand's photo subjects, the famous Zanzibar monkeys had so often been delegated to local dinner tables that a law had been passed that literally condemned to death anyone caught and/or convicted of killing any of the few remaining monkeys.

"Oh, just a few more sucks of my delicious dick," Ferdinand said and moved Bonjo's face into swifter, more rabbity, trips up and down, up and down. "Yes ... up and ... yes ... down and ... I'm ... going ... to come, you sexy black bastard. Yes! I do believe, I'm going to ... cum ... cum ... fucking cum ... real ... real ... soon."

Ferdinand's words might as well have been Jack's words, because Jack's cock and balls were primed to release Jack's cream.

"Aaaggghrruhgh!" Ferdinand said and socked the full length of his dick into Bonjo's face and kept it there by the steady push exerted by Filipino hips and by the steady pull of Ferdinand's handholds on Bonjo's head. "Aggghh ... agghrr ... grahhhh!"

Ferdinand's spermal bullets were invisible as they filled the nipple of the condom, lost deep within Bonjo's concealing throat, but the latex that took them was forced to stretch wide, in all directions, to contain it.

Jack's cum, though, was there for Jack to see as it erupted in heavy comets of slime that jettisoned from the literally pulsing mouth of his dick, became airborne until overcome by gravity, splash-landed on the dirt of the jungle-garden ground with splats that would surely have been audible if not for Ferdinand's ongoing climactic gutturals, not to mention Bonjo's animalistic sounds that vibrated the length of the Filipino dick held securely captured by the black kid's lips, mouth, and clutching throat.

If Bonjo's ejaculation was slightly later than what was managed by Jack or by Ferdinand, it was soon enough to allow Bonjo to enjoy it before Ferdinand's pleasure paled sufficiently to have the Filipino begrudge Bonjo any complementary enjoyment.

Bonjo's released cream, no way as impressive as the spurting gluey comets set loose from Jack's balls, were more like ore-heavy magma bubbled over the lip of some volcanic crater. His viscous goo flowed hot and heavy out of his cockmouth and down the neck of his black erection, where it was caught by Bonjo's still-stroking fingers and was smeared in pearly slime along the whole impressive length of the black boy's erection.

CHAPTER 5

"To our right, the house placed at Dr. Livingstone's disposal by the Sultan Seyyid Majid in 1866," Konoco Fassal said just a short way out of the hotel driveway.

The house sat behind a wall and outbuildings. It had three stories and a pointed red-tiled roof. Four rectangular green-shuttered windows looked out from both its second and third floors. Little of its lower level was visible except for one window and a door glimpsed through a closed gate. The outside of the house was mainly yellow stucco, relieved of monotony by a band of green that matched the green of the shutters and girdled the house between its ground and its upper two floors. There was a garage and a flagpole; the latter which flew the country's flag.

"The house was purchased in 1947 for use as a research laboratory with live-in facilities," Konoco said, the house now behind them. "Much of the original interior was gutted for renovation, making anything now inside of little historical significance."

A few minutes later, Konoco pointed out Maruhubi Palace, its ruins glimpsed, off to the left, through a symmetrical grove of high trees. "Its name comes from the man who once owned the land, the house built later by Seyyid Borghash for his harem. The house burned during the rein of Seyyid Hamound."

Jack successfully stifled a yawn.

Their next spot of interest were the caves at Mangapwani, a good many miles away and accessed via a roadway even more horrendously rutted than the main highway they left to get there.

The jungle had taken hold, undeterred now by the tramp of even the few sightseers who had made it that far in the best of times. Two flights of rough-hewn stone steps descended to a murky pool of stagnant water in the main cavern but didn't admit any fresh air. Hundreds, perhaps thousands, of slaves had once been packed together, at one and the same time, in that suffocating hole used by slave traders as a natural holding pen.

In contrast, the beach, just a few yards beyond, was a surprising and welcome relief.

"I should have brought swimming trunks," Jack said. He'd started sweating immediately after the comparative cool of the very early morning had given way to the greater heat that accompanied full sunrise. He hadn't stopped sweating since. "At least the breeze off the water is a pleasant change."

"Who says you need swimming trunks?" Konoco asked. "You see anyone here but us?"

While Konoco's invitation to cavort, naked as a jay, in the sand and surf, was enticingly inviting, Jack was uneasy about stripping naked before the Negro, not to mention made uneasy by even the possibility of the Negro's stripping naked before Jack. More than once, during their drive through the countryside, that morning, Jack had found himself with an erection less the result of the bumps and grinds, rocks and rolls, of the Land Rover over rough terrain, than the direct result of the Negro stud who sat in such close quarters with him.

"Nakedness, fresh air, and sunshine have an effect on me that can be a bit embarrassing," Jack said. Two men should be able to strip naked together and, in fact, did so every day of the year in locker rooms around the world, without either getting sexually aroused by the procedure. Even Jack could manage that, when the occasion demanded. On the other hand, Jack couldn't very well tell Konoco, "It's the prospect of your and my nakedness, along with the definitely non-locker-room fresh air and the sunshine that make me hornier than hell."

"As long as you've forewarned that your erection will have nothing to do with me, I promise not to be shocked when I see it," Konoco promised.

The black man crossed his arms across his chest and belly, took hold of the shirttail of his polo shirt, and lifted the material upward and off. What came uncovered was a miraculously well-chiselled physique: rectangular pectorals, rippled belly, charcoal nipples, knotted navel.

Jack stared. To cover what might be construed, and correctly so, as more interest than any straight man should have in another man's body, Jack said, "You come by all that muscle definition naturally, or do you have to work hard at it like the rest of us?"

"Little of both, I guess," Konoco said and didn't seem in the least embarrassed by how he might, or might not, have interpreted (or misinterpreted) Jack's interest. "Wonderful genes from dear dad. Not to mention the debt he and I both owe dear grandad who, after all, wouldn't have been such a favorite of his Arab master if not for the attractive way he was put together."

"Ah, yes, dear grandad," Jack said. His cock stirred in his pants and made him more ill at ease at even the idea of exposing such an unruly dick to Konoco, no matter how unfazed Konoco pretended to be by what might be in the offing.

"Mother's brothers, all three, are built like studly brick shithouses," Konoco said. He dropped his shirt to the sand. His hands poised on the waistband of his trousers.

Jack balanced between wanting to see the black man's cock on full display and worried how his white cock would react. Would Konoco really remain so blasÈ if Jack's cock emerged in painfully full erection?

"When I've a spare moment, I use the weight room at your hotel," Konoco said. "None of the fancy stuff that everyone

would use if they could afford it, these days, but a fairly
extensive selection of free weights from which to choose. So
...?"

Jack wasn't sure the question. "A needle pulling thread?"
he ventured in an attempt to defuse what, at least for him, was
a potentially explosive situation. "As a definition for sew, I
mean."

Konoco laughed. A nice laugh. Not too loud. Not too soft.
A pleasant, almost purr, accompanied by a display of even
white teeth and a slight squint of both eyes.

"Do love the American sense of humor!" he said. "But I
was referring to your taking a bit of sun. As in: So, how about
it?"

"I don't know," Jack said. His dick was definitely stiffer.

"Still worried that I'll take your boner as some kind of
assault on my manhood?"

"Sometimes I can't control the damned thing," Jack alibied.
"Sometimes, it simply has a life all its own, does things of its
own accord that for the life of me I can't figure, even in
situations not the least bit sexual."

"I know what you mean," Konoco said. "Take this, for
example."

He flattened his left hand atop the ridge his boner made
down his left pants leg. He splayed his fingers so his thumb
and forefinger fell to one side of the ridge, his other three
fingers to the left. The pressure exerted by all his fingertips
more fully emphasized the bas-relief of his obviously large and
circumcised cockhead.

"Actually, though, my boner isn't the result of any great
mystery," Konoco said. "I tell you that so you won't think me as
the sort of guy, any more than you are, who gets this big and
this hard when just stripped down for a bit of harmless skinny-
dipping. I've just a particular fondness for this particular beach,

because of some pleasing sexual experiences I've had here. My cock has difficulty separating those memories from the totally harmless reality."

He unclipped the metal fastener that kept the waistband of his trousers closed. He flipped up the metal tab that secured his zipper. He didn't physically slide the zipper tab down but rather pulled outward on the already slightly open material, on either side, to exert pressure from the top on down. As a result, the zipper widened from its top to its bottom and revealed, unhindered by any underwear, more and more of Konoco's muscled belly.

In finale, it opened over the dark curly strands that grew the base of Konoco's cockshaft and revealed just a fraction of his cockbase projected downward into the concealing leg of his trousers.

"I really do think I'll take a bit of sun, au-naturel," Konoco said and unceremoniously dropped his pants.

His released cock possessed enough stiffness to spring to an upright position before his washboarded belly and slap his cockhead loudly against his stomach, a good two inches above the attractive knot of his navel.

Jack had seen enough Negro cock, in and out of the bedroom, in and out of the locker room, to know it was purely and old-wives' tale that all Negro's had giant cocks. Some of the biggest dicks Jack had ever seen had belonged to cracker white boys. There was no doubt in Jack's mind, though, that if ever there was a stereotypically big-dicked black man, Konoco Fassal was he.

Konoco's circumcised cock, ebony velvet, thick-veined, wide-bellied, wide-backed, bulbous-tipped, and bulky, had a mouth that was more cleaver slash with dark-purple sides.

"We'll just ignore them," Konoco said. "My boner and yours."

Slaves

He stepped out of the pile made by his dropped pants, and he ran gracefully for the water. His naked ass was big, without being too big. Its twin cheeks, united along their mutually shared and now shifting crack, dimpled and undimpled provocatively as he got nearer and nearer the water.

Suddenly, Jack feared making too much of his own boner, and too much of Konoco's boner, by not stripping down and following Konoco into the water. Not following made it seem as if both erections needed to be concealed, because there was something genuinely a bit unsavory about the two of them. Why make more of them than how easily Konoco was prepared to explain them away?

Besides, Konoco had as much as issued a challenge by stripping down, presenting his stiff cock in devil-make-care attitude. Jack risked coming off decidedly up-tight by not accepting nudity and hards-on with the same air of joie de vivre as Konoco did.

Nonetheless, Jack felt uneasy dropping his pants, although he did drop them. It was a strange sensation, the uncertainty he felt, because he could usually pride himself on how easily he accepted his sexuality and the sexuality of others. Definitely something to do with the heat and the physical beauty (of Konoco and the island). Definitely something to do with Konoco seemingly so sexually liberated on an island where homosexuality was against the law. If Jack had seen it proven, by Ferdinand and Bonjo, in the garden-jungle, that Zanzibar laws were sometimes disobeyed with impunity, Jack was still made uneasy by even the idea of his own blatant flaunting of local authority in any situation that could possibly compromise the job he was being paid by Field Speer to do. Jack arrested for sexual misconduct could throw a mighty big monkey wrench into works that had taken Field a long time to put into place. Not to mention Field having gone to the bother of specifically warning Jack to consider Konoco police and/or government affiliated until Field determined otherwise.

Jack left his clothes in the sand and began his slow trot toward Konoco and the awaiting sea. He moved faster when he realized Konoco, in the water, faced the horizon. Maybe Jack could make the water before ...

Konoco turned, his hard cock visible, his balls lapped by sea foam formed by the water that broke around his black and muscular thighs and ass. He waved and yelled something that Jack couldn't understand because of the sudden loudness of the water. The pressure of the sea in motion knocked Konoco's legs out from beneath him, even as Jack watched, and black butt was bounced over the sand as far as the water line.

"Water is great!" Konoco said when Jack offered a hand to help him up. The Negro's black skin was all aglitter with salt crystals, water droplets, and quartz sand, all of which took sunlight and transformed it into all the colors of the rainbow.

Jack was helplessly excited by his nearness to the black man and to the black man's hard cock, by the wind and the salty spray, by the water sounds and the warmth of the sun, by the row of tall palms that lined the far edge of the beach.

Feeling his cock about to leak its preseminal response to all of the attending stimuli, Jack turned into the water and entered with a dive that penetrated the face of an incoming wave. The liquid was warm and all-encompassing. It took him into a womb-like existence where the only sounds were watery ones, except for the beat of his heart.

His torso broke the water and thrust upward into the brightness of the sunshine. He shook his head to free his hair of water and sand. He squeegeed his face with the palms of his hands and almost lost his balance in the breaking force of another wave.

There was unbelievable sensuousness in standing stark

naked in the swirling surf and blazing sun. The water was a constant caress, teasingly running up his legs, pulling away before actually making contact with his cock and balls, only to return to actually lap and tickle the hair of his scrotum before, in one last withdrawal and rush forward, drenching his whole cock and balls and knocking Jack on his ass.

The water tasted pleasantly salty.

Jack stood to brazen another breaking wave. He turned to say something to Konoco about how fun it was, no mention to be made of its undiluted sensuousness.

Konoco had left the water to talk to someone. Jack hadn't a clue who the someone was. Automatically, Jack dipped his boner in the surf, although Konoco unabashedly still sported his.

Konoco and the newcomer moved farther up the sand and sat facing the water. Konoco spotted Jack and waved. It wasn't a get your ass out of the water wave. It wasn't a we're in big trouble wave, either. It was merely a signal for Jack to continue right along in his enjoyment.

Initially, Jack figured to outlast the newcomer by enjoying the continuing pleasures of surf and sun until the guy returned to wherever it was from which he'd come. After awhile, though, it seemed unlikely the newcomer was prepared to exit any time soon.

While Konoco continued, quite nonchalantly to display his black boner for the world to see, Jack was less inclined to come unashamedly from the water sprouting the erection that continued to poke from the base of his belly. So much of an erection that some of the tidal currents, that sucked and whirled about it, often bent it so sharply in one direction or another that Jack thought for sure his dick was being snapped off at its thick base.

If Konoco's erection might be explained away to the newcomer, by Konoco going through the same reasoning he'd used with Jack, Jack was less comfortable with his own, "Damn, there's nothing more boner-producing than romping naked in the sun and surf!"

He moved deeper into the water, where he was sure, despite whatever the ongoing flow of current, he'd keep submerged from mid-chest down. He took hold of his stiff dick, beneath the water, and began beating his meat furiously.

No need for finesse, just a hard and steady whip of his dick to get his rocks off and get him out of the water, limp cock in the lead, before he was wrinkled as a prune by to much exposure to the water.

No need to fondle his balls. The constantly shifting water did that well enough, the drag on his nuts increased by the way the water constantly caught and held within the black hair that fuzzed his nuts.

One major oceanic sucking, after a particularly large swell broke on the beach, almost lifted Jack off his feet and vacuumed him out to sea. He successfully resisted only by leaning his full weight against the current, all the while beating, beating, beating his meat amidst the constant swirl of caressing current.

"Come on, baby," he encouraged his cock to provide cum for the great ocean asshole. His voice was pretty much lost among the sounds of the water. Since he could hardly hear himself, no way, no matter the quirks of acoustics, did what he said reach Konoco and the newcomer who might make the connection between what Jack said and what Jack did below the waterline. "All daddy wants is a little cum. Not even a whole lot. Just enough to go limp-dicked for as long as it takes to leave the water, walk the sand to my pants, and get my trousers on."

Slaves

Yes, there was something about the locale, the sun, the surf, as well as Jack's consistent pumping of his dick, that was conducive to speedy orgasm. So, Jack didn't have to wait all that long.

"Just a bit more, and we're home free," he said. He thought of imagining Ferdinand in the jungle-garden with Filipino cock sucked by hungry black boy, but he already had more stimulation than he really needed, because he ... was ... going ... to ... let ... his ... cum ... go.

He let it go, too.

"Yes!" he shouted triumphantly, his dick in full eruption.

Ropes of his cream exited the mouth of his dick, got caught in the swirl of the surf, and elongated into ropy steamers that twisted this way and that, some completely claimed by the tide, some curling back upon itself and catching within the netting of black pubic hair that grew Jack's underbelly.

"Milk dick, ... milk dick ... milk my big dick!" Jack chanted and continued to whip his meat free of each and every slug of his quickly elongating cum that he could coax from his nuts, up the tubing of his whipped dick, and out into the accepting surf.

His cock suddenly spent, the continuing swirl of the water suddenly an irritant to his hyper-sensitive dick, Jack still didn't feel free to exit the water until his cock was more noticeably drooped.

Vigorously, he rubbed his pubic bush to break the tenuous holds his stale sperm held there, and washed the last of his incriminating evidence in the obliging sea.

He stayed in the water even beyond the point, but that was because he wanted to be sure no tardy spunk remained holed up in his elephant-trunk dick. More embarrassing than presenting his boner to the stranger on the beach would be his presenting a soft dick that suddenly drooled stale cum, like a runny nose drooled snot.

Only when Jack was completely satisfied did he battle the riptide and gain a sufficient foothold on the beach to exit the water onto the sand.

He paused a few seconds, completely out of the water, to use his flattened palms to squeegee his body free of as much clinging liquid as possible. He couldn't very well dash on up and put on his clothes over his wet body without appearing a bit daft. Hopefully, what water he couldn't palm off would evaporate before he reached his clothes.

The gaze of both men was full on Jack's progress up the beach, Konoco's cock as black and as erect as ever. Jack managed a struggle through sand that seemed suddenly determined to impede his each and every step, as if to delay him until his cock stiffened again.

Jack preferred a beeline directly to his clothes, but both black men stood in greeting and interrupted Jack short of his objective. Actually, black "man" was a misnomer, as far as the newcomer. While Konoco obviously fit the bill, his companion seemed younger than Jack had imagined possible as first glimpsed from the distance of the water.

"My cousin, Ahmad," Konoco introduced.

Jack accepted Ahmad's outstretched hand and its friendly squeeze of greeting.

Ahmad was somewhere in the same indefinable age group into which Jack placed Bonjo-of-the-jungle-garden. Ahmad looked young but, like Bonjo, was probably older than he seemed. There was something decidedly juvenile about his close-cropped skullcap of tightly curled black hair, his expressively large and wide-spaced black eyes, his thin but slightly flared nose, and his full but not thick lips, that was completely belied by his obviously well-muscled body contained within his tight-fitting shirt and pants.

"The same cousin you were visiting when you first ran into

me at the museum?" Jack asked and let go of Ahmad's fingers.

"I've cousins all over the island," Konoco said and showed white teeth. "This one living in this section but wanting to go into the city. I told him he could ride with us, with your permission, but first wanted him to see the size of your boner when you hauled it from the water."

Not sure he'd heard correctly, Jack looked as flustered as he actually was.

Konoco laughed. Ahmad laughed. Their laughter was infectious, but Jack only managed an embarrassed smile.

"You mistook Ahmad's arrival as some kind of danger sign," Konoco divined, "and ruined the treat I had for him by knocking your cock about in the water even more than the surf could ever manage to do."

"Yes, well ..." Jack began but left it at that.

"Jack is the typical Zanzibar tourist," Konoco said to Ahmad. "Well, maybe typical only in that he's positive Zanzibar laws, against certain kinds of sexual acts, are strictly enforced."

"Never happen!" Ahmad pooh-poohed.

"Even if they were enforced, Jack," Konoco said, " and you just happened to do something in violation, you'd merely find yourself deported to the good old US of A."

"I'd just as soon not be deported, thank-you," Jack said. "So, I'd better get dressed."

Jack headed for his clothes. Always quick on sexual recovery, he knew his masturbation to climax in the waves wasn't going to keep him soft much longer, in the face of Konoco's unabashed sexual innuendo.

"Wait for a bit more water to dry," Konoco said and followed after. "Here, let me wipe some of the wet from your back."

The flat of his hand travelled the width of Jack's back, once, then twice, then a final time that slid large black fingers along the beginning curves of Jack's ass. All the while, Jack stood, holding his pants but not putting them on.

"In the States, were I to turn around and grab your big black dick, I'd be acquitted of any wrong doing on the grounds of entrapment," Jack said.

"On Zanzibar, were you to turn around and grab my big black dick, I'd merely say, 'Thank-you!'" Konoco said. "You know the sex I told you had occurred on this very beach, the memories of which supposedly caused my boner in the first place?"

"I vaguely recall, yes." Jack's recollection was anything but vague.

"It was sex between Ahmad and me. Not once, but several times. True, Ahmad?"

"True, yes, cousin," Ahmad confirmed.

"Surprised, Jack? Shocked, Jack?" Konoco asked, his smile wider.

"Surprised only in that I figured the laws likely kept such stuff in check, or deeply undercover. Obviously, I was wrong."

"Finally, he sees the light, Ahmad! There's hope yet."

"Hope for what?" Jack asked curiously. His cock was visibly elongated and made him nervous.

"Hope that you might be enticed into a bit of mutually pleasurable fun and games," Konoco said. "From the very first moment I spotted you walking the aisles of our museum, playing with that hard dick of yours so evident in your pants, I said to myself, 'Konoco,' I said, 'wouldn't you like to get your black hands on that white boy's white cock and white ass?' Didn't I tell you about the studly white boy I met up with in the museum, Ahmad?"

"'Handsome as hell. Studly as hell. Hung as all hell!' That's what you said," Ahmad agreed.

"The question, of course, is whether Jack is at all interested in any of this," Konoco defined. "Granted, Jack was sequestered for a bit with Professor Mider who likes cock as much as the next queer, Mider as nervous as Jack about the possible consequences, but not so nervous that he hasn't slipped on not one, but several occasions."

Jack wondered if that shouldn't be reported to Field who, after all, had the most to lose if all the time and effort taken to get Carl in place was suddenly screwed up by Carl being deported.

"I'll bet money that Carl," Konoco decided, "couldn't control his hunger when exposed to even the possibility of a big-cocked American tourist. Were you able to fend him off, Jack, or is that a fair question? If it's unfair, how about this one: Was your earlier boners, between here and the city, merely from being jostled about in the car?"

"You need more of an answer than my big cock getting bigger and bigger even as I stand here?"

"Is your cock getting bigger and bigger?" Jack asked. "Turn around and let me see."

Jack obliged and lowered his handful of pants to give Jack and Ahmad a good look.

"That something I'm really happy to see," Konoco said. "Because, while I had the gut feeling we might be of like mind, as far as attractive men and their cocks and assholes go, it's sometimes hard to judge. Let's face it, Jack, you're a stud from the word go who would have most any lady's cunt drooling over having at your big cock. For all I really knew, you might actually preferred that."

"Not likely."

"Never once tempted?"

"Not once."

"Nor I. Ahmad, now, swings both ways, don't you, Ahmad? Were this back in the good old days, when tourists flocked here in droves, Ahmad would be hauling in money hand over fist. Pleasing men, when they wanted pleasing. Pleasing women, when they wanted pleasing. Alas, such good times, are no longer on Zanzibar, and Ahmad is relegated to performing for free with local sluts, and/or with his own hand, and/or with his horny uncle."

"This all seems a bit ... out in the open," Jack finally described it. He was no longer talking just Konoco and Ahmad's candidness but the vast and empty beach which him feel particularly exposed and vulnerable.

"Few people come here," Konoco said. "To this beach, I mean, although the same could be said for coming to the island, period. As for this beach, in particular, the locals definitely prefer beaches closer to home. This beach, beautiful as it is, popular as it once was with unsuperstitious foreign tourists, has many ghosts for the average Zanzibari. It's too close to the Mangapwani caves, and the slaving practices that went on there. Many a Zanzibar Negro, in fact the vast majority, not nearly as well-disposed toward their Arab masters as members of my family once were."

"There could be anyone in those trees," Jack reminded. "With cameras. With telephoto lenses."

"Could be green cheese on the moon," Konoco said, "but is there? Unless, of course, left by one of your Yankee moon-walking astronauts."

"Let's go to the Kidichi Baths," Ahmad said. Nonchalantly, he played with his cock through the crotch of his trousers. By all evidence, Jack had somehow lucked upon two stellarly stereotypically well-hung black men, at one and the same time.

"Yes," Konoco agreed. "Let's do."

"The Kidichi Baths?" Jack wanted to know.

"Of some historical interest to someone, like yourself, in that they are a part of the island's early Arab slave-trade heritage," Konoco said. "Of even more interest because they offers a privacy far less threatening than these wide-open spaces."

CHAPTER 6

The Baths were on the way back to the city but no more easily reached than any of the other historical sites deteriorated from rampant neglect. Twice, Jack thought they had the wrong road, although road was a misnomer, the jungle having so thoroughly obliterated the original track. At one spot, a sixteen-foot tree grew in the center of the wheel ruts, and driving around it was such a tight squeeze that there were resulting scratch marks to the Land Rover. Although taken with the scratch marks already there, they weren't all that outstanding.

"Built circa 1850 by Seyyid Said Ben Sultan," Konoco began his tourist-guide spiel before the baths were sighted, "for his Persian wife, Princess Shehrazid, granddaughter of Fateh ali Shaid, the Shah of Persia."

The Baths materialized through, around, beside, and amongst the undergrowth. Konoco's preview was far more glorious than the actual crumbling array of domes, of various sizes, in the middle of seeming nowhere.

"Pick a building at random," Konoco said. "One pretty much the same as the other, except for a bit of difference in size, except for a bit of variance in the surviving (at least surviving when last I looked), Persian-style stuccos to be found inside."

"Door number three," Jack said, although he suspected, and correctly, that neither of his companions got his insinuated connection to a popular game show on American TV.

"Good as any," Konoco said and headed in that direction. "Making plenty of noise as we approach, please, if only because the shady interiors once offered sanctuary to all sorts of wildlife out for a respite from the brain-baking noonday sun."

Slaves

The structure looked even more rundown when they reached it.

"Ahmad, do take a quick look inside," Konoco insisted. "Better you suffer a snake bite than I try to explain how an American tourist expired on the spot. You, after all, the one who recommended the accommodations."

Jack was about to protest Ahmad acting as guinea pig, but Ahmad was less reluctant to assume the responsibility and was through the low doorway before Jack could say anything to stop him.

"Not to worry," Konoco said. "Really. Not nearly as dangerous as I might have led you to believe. Anything that once might have sought shelter inside has long since expired inside some local cooking pot. And, I do mean anything."

Which didn't keep Jack from worrying when Ahmad seemed longer inside than seemed absolutely necessary.

"Maybe eaten by the last wild boar on Zanzibar," Konoco suggested. "If there is such a thing." His accompanying smile labelled his suggestion no more serious than he'd meant it to be.

A few seconds later, Ahmad appeared.

"Jack was sure you'd been dealt with by the ghosts of the place," Konoco said by way of greeting his cousin.

"I'm fine," Ahmad assured Jack, since there was no reason to believe his cousin had been genuinely concerned.

"Ahmad shall lead the way," Konoco said. "Jack through next. I'll bring up the rear and fight off ... ghosts ... or whatever."

The entryway was as low as it looked, Jack having to squat to get through. There was only a short passageway that opened into the dimly lit interior of one domed room.

Jack came unbent. Obviously, Ahmad had done a bit of housekeeping, but there were still webs in the high corners and high along the ceiling and walls. Jack didn't want to meet up with whatever had spun such gossamer veils. He'd once seen a tarantula and didn't like the memory.

"The owners of even those long-neglected webs, eaten along with everything else," Konoco said, having read Jack's mind. "Rather tasty, like chicken, once you fire off the fur and bake the rest of the spider over an open fire."

Jack shuddered.

"So, this is stucco decorated in the Persian style," Jack said, wanting to change the subject. The designs upon which he commented were weathered and mostly dissolved by humidity, neglect, and time.

"At this rate of deterioration, nothing will be left in a couple of years," Konoco said. "An island anxious to promote tourism should make a better effort to preserve what it has, by way of its unique heritage, wouldn't you think? Plenty of islands with palm trees, white beaches, blue oceans, and rampant poverty. However, most everyone on Zanzibar will be quite happy to see all of this evidence of Arab domination crumble to dust and disappear completely."

"Over this way," Ahmad said and motioned toward another low doorway.

Jack followed, and Konoco again brought up the rear.

Jack tried to imagine how the place must have been in its prime, alive with the presence of a princess and her attendants. Now, stone troughs that once carried cool, perfumed water, only held dry, sinus-clogging dust. It was hard to imagine any of the baths ever having been any more than their present piles of stucco flaking like dandruff.

A lone window filtered milky light through a lattice of stone, dirt, and still intact web-work.

"Private enough?" Konoco asked. "Granted, every cupola might be electronically bugged, but surely that's a bit too

involved a plot to catch one gay tourist who'd return to the
States with horror tales of human rights violations on Zanzibar,
don't you think?"

Probably, but was it too involved a trap to trip up Field
Speer and what he, with Carl Mider and Jack's help, was all
about?

Konoco reached into his rear pocket and pulled out his
wallet which he opened to count out a few local bills. He
handed the money to Ahmad who immediately pocketed it and
began to undress.

"Wait!" Jack said but suspected things had been taken out
of his hands.

He was faced with the dilemma of protesting too much. A
fate of one Shakespearean character of whom it was accused,
"The lady doth protest too much." Would any normal man, with
even an inclination toward gay sex, confronted with the
scenario Konoco and Ahmad offered, opt out?

Jack fished his pocket for his wad of American dollars.

"I want to give Ahmad something," he said. "Sorry, but I
haven't a clue how much."

"Just remember what I once told you about the value of just
one US dollar on present-day Zanzibar," Konoco reminded.

Jack counted off five ones. It seemed pitifully little,
considering what was charged by the ugliest kid who peddled
his cock and ass on any American street corner. Both Ahmad
and Konoco prime specimens of manhood.

Jack handed the money to Ahmad who looked to Konoco
who nodded his okay for Ahmad to take it.

"You'll have to keep your mouth shut that Jack is quite so
generous," Konoco told his cousin. "Or, you'll have to fight off
the men eager to cash in."

"Actually, he doesn't have to do anything for the money,"
Jack said. "It's a gift."

Konoco laughed.

"Jack, Jack, Jack," Konoco chanted and laughed some more. "Oh, yes, I suppose Ahmad does sell his body for the money. He has to do it for the money, or he'd likely starve. As well as would his mother. As well as would his brother. But he doesn't do it with you just for the money, only in that he has to do it for the money. If he didn't have to do it for the money, he'd do it with you for free, because he wants to do it with you. We're from a long line of cock-suckers and bum-fuckers, aren't we, Ahmad? All the way back to grandaddy and his Arab stud. You're the best thing to come our way in a helluva long time."

"Should I settle up now with you, too?"

"Later," Konoco dismissed with a wave of his hand and wished he wasn't so financially strapped, like Ahmad, as to be unable to offer up his sexual services for free.

Ahmad, confident the business was out of the way, fully removed his shirt.

As with his first spotting of Bonjo, in the garden-jungle, Jack was amazed by how nicely developed, physically, Ahmad was for someone who looked as young as he looked. Possibly the difficulty in getting enough to eat on Zanzibar had merely stripped all its youth of unseemly excess fat and flesh. What remained was something exquisitely hard, as if carefully chiselled in black marble with totally no waste. Ahmad's pectorals were perfect circles, separated by a pectoral cleavage not deep but no less well-defined than it would have been if it had been. Each pectoral had its quarter-sized nipple, black against black.

His stomach was taut, possibly even concave, as stretched between his two prominent hipbones. It was a cobbled stomach, like some roadways were rippled with paving stones: his belly an intricate jigsaw puzzle of irregularly bulged abdominal muscles that seemed a perfect fit. His navel was a mere dimple that winked ever so slightly as he unfastened his pants and bent slightly as they dropped around his feet.

His cock was large. Not as long as Konoco's cock. Not as long as Jack's cock. Large nonetheless. It was nearly as thick as Konoco's cock and might have been as thick as Jack's. It was jacketed with an uncut foreskin that turtlenecked its bulbous cockhead which had shot through it, in cock's full erection, like a shirt cuff shot through a suit-jacket sleeve.

Each of his balls was a handful, contained in a scrotum hung in such a way as to have a double chin, his nuts suspended within the first, the second draped immediately below.

He had nice legs and a nice butt.

He was hairless except for a small patch of sporadic curly strands at the base of his dick.

"See the family resemblance?" Konoco asked and peeled off his shirt. He undid his pants, dropped them, put his still-hard cock back on display, and simultaneously stepped out of his shoes and out of his dropped trousers.

Under any other similar circumstances, Jack would have been in Seventh Heaven. One of his most ongoing fantasies was to be sexually sandwiched between two such black studs. He'd jacked off to that fantasy, more than once, upon first hearing that he was coming to Zanzibar. Never, though, had he believed, in his wildest dreams, that the fantasy could be brought so close to the reality.

If only he were just on Zanzibar to research a paper. If only he weren't part of something so much bigger and so complex that it had taken virtual years for Carl Mider to get into place. If Jack's part was less complicated than Carl's, it would take valuable time to replace Jack if Jack goofed up. Everything in place, here and now, Jack out of the equation, booked by the local police for having been sexually sandwiched between

Konoco and Ahmad, would see Field's whole plan needing revamped. Would the authorities even let Field back into the country to replay his present role of keeping everyone's attention focused elsewhere than on what was really going on?

"What say we start without you?" Konoco suggested. "You feel free to join in, if and when."

Jack was the only one with clothes on, even though the obvious hardness of his cock said, as much as anything, that he would prefer being naked.

"We should have rubbers," Jack said. He'd been hired by Field for his intelligence, among other attributes, and was determined to use it. He could usually trust his intuition, and it told him this seemed too clever for entrapment. How could anyone on Zanzibar, but Carl and Field, know he was gay? Did the Zanzibar authorities, even now, have a black woman in reserve should Jack prove straight?

"We have rubbers, don't we, Ahmad?" Konoco said. He squatted for his pants, and Jack actually thought the Negro's big dick was going to poke its owner in the chin. "Swedish-made, because the Swedes are one of the few who haven't deserted Zanzibar as a cheap tourist spot. The Swedes having their fair share of queers. And, if they didn't, what straight Swede would really care if the rubbers he so graciously handed out are sometimes used for a cock's passage up male mouth, or up male ass, instead of up female mouth, up female ass, or up cunt?"

He showed Jack the blue-plastic wrapper of a rubber. Ahmad's condom was packaged in white.

Not to be outdone, Jack produced a lubricated Trojan, although he thought it would have been more apropos to have had a Sheik.

"We've rubbers to spare," Konoco said, a pat of his pants pocket indicating more in reserve.

Slaves

"So, how do we do this?" Jack asked. He was committed. They knew it, too. If theirs was an elaborate plan to trap him, he was trapped. If he wished his actions controlled more by his brain than by his cock, he had to deal with the reality of being turned on beyond belief by these two black-stallion studs.

"We do this anyway you want to do this," Konoco said. "Aren't I right, Ahmad, that the man paying the money calls the tune?"

"Right!"

If Jack was in this with both feet, both balls, his big cock, and his tight ass, he might as well make fantasy fact. God only knew when he'd have the chance ever again. Certainly not on Zanzibar which Jack never planned to visit again, even if he would be allowed back in after his part in Field's proposed plan.

"Surely, you've a preference?" Konoco asked. "Because, while I'd like nothing better than to get my hard black dick fucked up your white ass, I've the quandary of, also, wanting to get my black butt fucked by your big white horse-cock."

Jack could be faintly amused by how their three-way might never get started, because all of them were too versatile to decide who would do what to whom.

"Ahmad?" Konoco tried before suggesting they draw straws.

"I want this white stud's cock rammed deep up my ass," Ahmad said. "Can you do that for me, white stud? Make me squeal as if I'm a stuck pig, your cock a steely spit."

"Sure," Jack said and peeled off his shirt. His dime-size nipples had tack-hard centers.

He dropped his pants and stepped out of them and out of his shoes. The floor was surprisingly cool against the soles of his bare feet.

"Big hard dick," Ahmad said. "Cousin Konoco said it was, and he didn't lie."

"I'll need a moment to get it rubberized," Jack said,

squatted for his pants and for the handkerchief in a front
pocket. "Damned cock leaks like sixty when I get excited. I'm
excited."

"Let's see it leak a bit more," Konoco said. "Stroke it and
make it ooze."

"Yeah," Ahmad agreed.

Since his dick had already grown wet with its preseminal
goo, Jack did as instructed. The noose formed by his index
finger and thumb milked his dick of more wet which overflowed
his cockmouth.

"I've never seen such white-cock leaker," Ahmad said and
licked his lips.

"Heard people say there isn't a better lubricant for a fuck
than white-cock goo," Konoco said, moving in really close to
Jack and squatting for a better look.

Ahmad squatted on Jack's other side.

"Can I touch?" Ahmad asked. "Just enough to get a small
sample on my fingers."

Konoco ran a hand up the back of Jack's leg. His fingers
slid in between Jack's thighs and tickled the hair on Jack's
balls.

Jack's cock leaked more goo. Ahmad touched the sluggish
run of liquid, rubbed his fingers together, and hummed
appreciation, as if he'd discovered the secret that turned base
metal to gold.

"Slick," he said. "Really slick. And smooth. Really
smooth."

"Rubbers may be safer, but are they really more fun?"
Konoco asked with a sigh. He took hold of Jack's balls, as if
both nuts were the single teat of a cow's udder, and he gave a
gentle, stretching tug.

"I've never had unsafe sex," Jack said.

"Not likely to have it, either, I suppose, on an island off the

Slaves

coast of AIDS-spawning Africa," Konoco said and gave yet
another tug on Jack's nuts. After which, he enjoyed the latest
drool from Jack's erection.

Ahmad claimed more lubricant from the head of Jack's
cock, foamed it between his rubbing thumb and forefinger.

"Best rubber up that drooly white dick of yours, white boy,"
Konoco said, "before you suddenly find either Ahmad or my butt
sat down over it, all of the way to your big white balls, without
you ever knowing what happened."

Jack used his hanky to soak up the readily available wet, as
well as whatever he could milk from the neck of his cock.
When his cock was dry enough, he capped it with condom and
rolled latex all of the way down his cockshaft to his balls. By
the time his dick was completely raincoated, Konoco's cock was
rubberized, too. As Ahmad would head the daisy-chain, he put
his condom back in his pocket and left his cock bare.

"Give me a minute to get my rubber wet," Konoco said.
"Unlike yours, mine is dry as a desert."

Jack expected Konoco to spit in his hand, smear the
resulting slime along the length of his rubberized dick. Maybe
even ask Jack to give his dick enough of a suck to drool the
shaft with sufficient saliva for a butt-fuck. Instead, Konoco took
hold of his black cock, pulled it slightly out from his black belly,
bent from the waist, and lowered his face all of the way to the
head of his dick, where his mouth clamped over and took hold.

"Jesus!" Jack said. As big as Jack's dick was, he'd never
quite managed the dexterity to eat his own meat, and it wasn't
for lack of trying.

"A bit of double-jointedness runs in the family," Ahmad said
and did a quick head dip as far as the head of his own cock.
He didn't linger but bobbed back up. "I'm thinking of maybe
sucking my dick just at the moment your white cock, up my
black ass, has me creaming my load. Maybe get my dick

sucked so deep inside my throat that I can see between my legs, beyond my compact balls, and spot your black-haired white balls as they pump your steamy cum through your dick and into the rubber-rammed depth up my butt."

"Look a little farther in that direction, and you'll be able to see my nuts, too," Konoco said, up from lathering his rubberized dick with spit. "And guess what my nuts will be doing?"

"Let's get my asshole familiar what your cock can do," Jack suggested, "before that spit bath you've given your condom evaporates and you have to do your human-pretzel routine one more time."

"Me first," Ahmad said, turned his ass in Jack's direction, his own hands on his own muscled buns to widen their shared crack and reveal the startlingly tiny doorway to his ready and willing asshole.

Jack stepped up, hooked the shaft of his cock with his thumb, and weighted his dick from its vertical to a horizontal position that slid the lubrication-slicked nippled tip of his rubber down the crack from the small of Ahmad's back to a direct poke of the anal target area.

It was a backward thrust of Ahmad's ass that buried his asshole over half of Jack's cock in one big gulp. It was hard for Jack to tell, by Ahmad's resulting, "Aggghhhrrr!", whether or not the young Negro was pleased by what he'd done or simply realized too late he'd too quickly taken on more than his butt could immediately handle. The question answered when, hot on the tail of his asshole swallowing half of Jack's dick, a second bucking of Ahmad's hips force-fed the other half of Jack's dick in to join the first.

"Ugh! Ugh!" It was Jack's turn to do a bit of grunting. Ahmad's ass was exquisitely tight. So tight it was hard for Jack to imagine how so much of Jack's cock could have been so thoroughly thrust into it in so short a time. His hands anchored to Ahmad's hips and held on, the pleasure making him dizzy.

"I should have warned you that my family is known for the tightness of its assholes, too," Konoco said, so close behind Jack that his hard nipples pressed tack-like indents into Jack's back. "Another genetic key to grandaddy's popularity with his Arab master, passed down to grandaddy's descendants to this very day."

"I can well imagine how that Arab might have been impressed enough to keep your grandaddy around," Jack said. His voice was decidedly breathless.

"The family assholes sometimes get cock off just by anal chomping, and a bit of anal vibration," Konoco said. "Whomever's lucky dick not having to do a damned thing. But, I don't want Ahmad's butt to show you any of that particular magic, because I want to show you how it's done sometime when your white dick is fucked up my behind. So you might think about blocking me a bit more time, somewhere up the line."

Konoco's hand aimed his hard cock directly at the floor, the strain exerted to keep it there seemingly enough to soon pop the cock from its stalwart anchorage. Not that the pain was sufficient to soften his dick, because his cock remained rock-hard.

Konoco's cock approach to Jack's rosy-red asshole wasn't down Jack's asscrack, from backbone to pucker, but upward, from Jack's balls to anal opening. At first, Konoco's cock thrust between Jack's thighs, the spit-wet cockhead cool where it jabbed the back of Jack's testicles, Jack thinking the studly Negro had missed the target completely.

Konoco, though, hadn't missed anything. He knew exactly what he was doing, and where his cock was going. Which included wrapping both of his arms around Jack, his hands slipping in between Jack's belly and Ahmad's ass, his flattened palms sliding up Jack's belly to Jack's chest to cover both of Jack's hard-centred nipples.

By edging his hips back just a bit at a time, Konoco guided his cockhead along that section of Jack's body that connected Jack's scrotum to the lower beginnings of Jack's asscrack. Edging his hips back farther, yet, saw the head of Konoco's cock slipped into Jack's asscrack at the crack's lower end. It was then only a matter of Konoco applying just enough forward pressure, of cockhead to asscrack, to counteract the stiffness of his dick that wanted, immediately, to spring Konoco's big cock into a fully vertical erection before the black man's belly. A fraction of an inch at a time, Konoco's cock, like the big hand of a clock, jerked closer and closer to contact with Jack's pucker.

"Ahhhh, yes!" Konoco and Jack harmonized at one and the same time.

Lest his starched dick provide even one additional jerk toward vertical to take it out of proper alignment, Konoco's hips thrust forward and subjected the rubber-nippled tip of his prick to the gummy gulp of Jack's sphincter.

"You want it slow and easy?" Konoco asked, his head resting on Jack's left shoulder. "You want it hard and fast?"

"I wouldn't want my asshole ripped," Jack said. Which suddenly seemed a genuine possibility. Never had his asshole seemed so tight, never had a cock about to slide completely into it seemed so big. Although he had taken bigger ...

Konoco, apparently, at least for the moment, a better judge of what Jack's asshole could or couldn't take with safety, gave Jack the rest of Konoco's huge black cock in one unstoppable rush that slammed Konoco's belly hard against Jack's ass and swung Jack's belly into a much tighter fit against Ahmad's cock-plugged butt.

"Fucking, shit!" Jack said, after the fact. His asshole had

taken Konoco's force-fed cock with hardly a protest until after the cock was fully embedded. After it happened, Jack's rectum decided it had been taken advantage of, taken by unfair surprise, and went through a series of protesting squeezes that tried to mash Konoco's cock to nothingness, anal ripples trying their best to shit out what was being mistaken as residue from a good month of acute constipation.

"Oh, I do see it's just not members of my immediate family with well-honed assholes," Konoco said, thoroughly enjoying the discomfort of his phallic sword fully rammed into what put on such a good show of being a way-too-small sheathe.

The three men, united into a three-headed and six-legged chimera, didn't do much of anything for awhile except become accustomed to being stuck and sticking.

Jack wished for a mirror to show him the black-on-white-on-black picture the three men presented. His mental image of the effect, named for a famous American cookie, was enough to send another sensation of pleasure cascading through him to spasm his ass yet again along the entire length of Konoco's deeply penetrated inches.

"Mmmmmyyyy," Konoco admitted to the additional pleasure he experienced as a result of Jack's ass still not having learned that it had what it had with nothing it could do about it.

Jack's next rush of pleasure was the result of nothing physical. Not Konoco's cock up his butt. Not his cock up Ahmad's butt. It was from the danger of this possibly being a trap, now to be interrupted by local authorities rushing in and hauling his queer ass off to jail for having committed lewd and lascivious unnatural acts. On the other hand, it seemed more and more unlikely that things would actually have been allowed to get this far if the purpose was purely to trick Jack into a sexually compromising position.

"What say I start the train moving from this end?" Konoco

suggested, his cock having finally ridden Jack's ass into submission.

Konoco surrendered some of his well-won victory by pulling his cock out of the hole that he'd just made take it. When only his rubberized cockhead remained slotted within Jack's asshole, Konoco's hands slipped down to Jack's hips and exerted a slight pull that was Jack's cue.

Jack's lower body pulled his large white cock out of Ahmad's tight black ass. As more and more of his white dick returned to daylight, Jack's asshole simultaneously rode back along the same length of Konoco's black cock that had so recently been let go. By the time Jack's cock had only its rubber-nippled head jammed into Ahmad's butt, Jack's ass was once again completely seated over Konoco's hard dick.

"Come on, Ahmad," Jack encouraged. His hands already on the young boy's hips, they exerted the pressure that started the swing of Ahmad's black ass back along each and every inch of Jack's stiff dick.

All three men had done little but move the lower parts of their bodies, so their present positioning gave the appearance of three question marks turned upside down . To come out of that grouping, Ahmad's hips began a forward shift, his asshole reluctantly expelling inch after inch after inch of white-man cock. All of which Ahmad couldn't help but find exceptionally thrilling.

His butt pulled off white meat to the point where, once again, it was only rubberized white cockhead locked by Ahmad's gumming sphincter, Ahmad ceased all movement and waited while Jack's cock came forward and slid right back into Ahmad's eagerly awaiting ass.

Jack's belly once again nestled tightly against the perfect fit offered by the curves of Ahmad's butt, Jack's ass suddenly holding only the fat head of Konoco's cock, Konoco's cock came forward and filled the same asshole that had just let it go.

The process was repeated. Repeated again. Until each man had a mind's-eye picture of how things went. It was important they know, and get the feel of the right way, because one man out of sync in any daisy-chain could spoil the flow by letting a cock slip suddenly and completely free. While the replacement of any such wayward dick could be pleasurable, there was more pleasure in the uninterrupted slow and easy, well-coordinated, steady buildup of ecstasy that came from a more skillfully choreographed dance.

As each man became more familiar with the rhythm required, the speed was picked up a bit, then picked up a bit more

On one inward slide of Jack's cock within Ahmad's butt, the black boy opted to put his hands on his thighs and bend forward. Not only in preparation for having his mouth near his hard dick when it finally exploded, so he could suck his lips tightly over his cock and suck up each and every drop of his cum, but because it allowed him better balance as the threesome fucked into even higher gear.

Jack had a variation of his own that he'd planned from the start. He leaned forward in a cupping of Ahmad's bent-forward body and ran both his hands on a search-and-find mission that resulted in Jack's successful fisting of Ahmad's hard cock (or, at least a fisting of as much of it as was humanly possible), and a grabbing of Ahmad's hairy balls.

"Ooooohhhhahhhhh!" Ahmad responded to the additional assault on his body. He'd purposely not touched his own cock, with his hands or with his mouth, because he'd feared how any resulting pleasure, combined with the sheer ecstasy of white cock slid in and out of his rear, might thrust him too hard and too fast toward orgasm. He was even more fearful of those consequences now that he felt the dual-forked jolt of electricity that surged, from contact point of white hand on black cock and from contact point of white fingers on black scrotum, to rocket throughout each and every fiber of Ahmad's thoroughly white-fucked being.

Jack had troubles of his own keeping his swelling passion in check. After all, this was a living and breathing fantasy made real. Previously, he'd only imagined it — when he'd masturbated; when he'd fucked or been fucked by white cock, or by Spanish cock, or by Asian cock; when he'd been fucked by black cock, although never a real second black man present — until now.

Now: truly wondrous! Now: so much more intense than any illusion. Never did Jack remember, and he was a pro at fucking and getting fucked, with a roll call of experienced partners under his belt, feeling so quickly taken to those heights of ecstasy from which there was nowhere to go but the fall into gut-exploding oblivion.

"I know how, from the start, I found you sexy," Konoco said and punctuated with breathless little grunts. "I know how, from the start, I found your ass sexy. I know how, from the start, I found your cock sexy. But fucking sexy you, my cock up your sexy ass, your sexy cock up Ahmad's sexy black backside, is genuinely too fucking sexy to believe!"

Konoco's cock pulled out, and Jack's ass rolled back down over it, as Jack's cock slid out of Ahmad's asshole, as Ahmad's asshole then rolled back over Jack's erection.

"You get me hot, white boy," Konoco said. "You get me real hot. You get me hotter than this black man can ever remember being hot before. And I do mean ... hot-hot hot."

Ahmad couldn't have spoken if he'd wanted. He concentrated too totally on keeping his raging pleasure from overtaking him and sending him into cataclysmic orbit before Jack's nuts blasted off up his butt. Jack was paying, and whether or not Ahmad got his own black-boy's rocks off didn't matter. Ahmad was disturbed that this white man's cock was better than any other white cock ever fucked up Ahmad's butt before it. If Ahmad could attribute some of the specialness of the three-way in progress to Konoco's glowing reports of Jack beforehand, to Konoco's cock-fucking Jack's white ass at that very moment, even as Jack's cock fucked Ahmad's ass, that still wasn't any excuse for the horrible mistake Ahmad made if he interrupted the flow and kept Jack's nuts from letting go and blasting their heavy load of rubber-basting cream when they could have.

Worst of all, Ahmad knew Konoco would be disappointed if Ahmad spoiled things. Konoco having wanted sex, any kind of sex, with the handsome American from the first minute he'd seen Jack in the museum. Not only that, but Konoco had arranged for Ahmad to join in, expecting Ahmad to exercise the same control the boy so expertly managed whenever Konoco and Ahmad had sex. Konoco felt Ahmad and he could really give Jack the American's monies' worth, because Konoco, who would have preferred the luxury of sex with Jack for free, wanted Jack knowing money had bought something here, on Zanzibar, that couldn't be bought anywhere else.

And here Ahmad was, on the very verge of orgasm. The unfairness almost overwhelmed him.

If only Jack hadn't taken hold of Ahmad's cock, or squeezed Ahmad's balls. If only Jack would turn loose of Ahmad's cock and balls, even now. Except, Ahmad was already too near climax to be interrupted by the removal of Jack's hands. Just the continued pump of Jack's cock up Ahmad's butt was all Ahmad needed as the last shove that teetered him over the edge into ...

"Oh, no!" Ahmad voiced his despair as another bang of Jack's cock into Ahmad's prostate, and the cock's careening slide by, pulled the trigger that set Ahmad's bullets on their way.

Automatically, Ahmad's face closed the distance between his mouth and his cockhead. Not quick enough, though, to capture the first spermal slug that pasted Ahmad's chin and dribbled it before his open mouth set down atop the blast-off zone and gulped each and every ensuing ounce of pulsing, pulsing, seemingly endless pulsing, heavy cream.

Jack was so caught in his own near-peaking experience, he didn't have a clue that Ahmad, head over exploding dick, was rupturing Ahmad's black-boy nuts. Jack's passion-clogged brain imagined the sudden rippling strangulation of his cock by Ahmad's butt as yet more proof-positive that Zanzibar asshole, in general, was pretty terrific,and that Ahmad's asshole, specifically, was pretty damned wonderful, too.

"I'm going to cum!" Jack said, although it came out more like, "Immmmmguungcummmmm!"

However he said it, it meant one and the same. He socked his cock full-depth up Ahmad's spasming rear end, his momentum pushing Ahmad's exploding dick even farther into the black boy's sucking face. Jack's nuts, hoisted high against the base of his dick, blasted wad after wad of spunk to join the preseminal slime that had veneered the interior of the condom's rubber nipple before them.

The domino effect had Ahmad's asshole, spasming from Ahmad's orgasm, bringing Jack to climax; Jack's asshole, spasming from Jack's orgasm, bringing Konoco to climax.

Konoco was the most surprised, in that he'd figured to make this fuck last and last and last. That it hadn't lasted nearly as long as he'd wanted, expected, or planned, was so deeply disappointing — who knew when he might have another go at this white stud's asshole? — that it registered even as his rocks sped cum through his juice-contributing prostate, up and out his cock, and filled the rubber plugged deep up Jack's ass.

Konoco hunched farther over Jack's buttocks, reached

beyond Jack to overlap Jack's hands anchored on Ahmad's prominent hipbones.

"Oooheeeiii!" Konoco squealed and fed his rubber wad after hot-and-heavy wad of pearly male cream. He bit Jack's neck, but not hard enough to break the skin, and held on for dear life as his body rocketed, through and through, with unbearable ecstasy.

CHAPTER 7

They dropped Ahmad in the old city.

Field Speer appeared through the main doors of the hotel just as Konoco and Jack drove up. He stopped to watch Jack exit the car.

"Ah, Mr. Mallard-like-the-duck!" he called. "Or, should I say, Jack/jack-like-the-whatever? Whatever have you been up to that sees the Zanzibar police involved?"

"Beg your pardon?" Jack was genuinely confused.

"That is Mr. Fassal in the car, isn't it? Or, should I say Corporal Konoco Fassal, Zanzibar Police?"

Jack turned to Konoco, frankly agape. "You're a cop?" What might have sounded not only possible but probable, just a few hours before, was now mind-boggling.

"Get in!" Konoco said and didn't invite argument.

"Under arrest, Jack?" Field asked. "I know some important people on this hellhole upon whom I can call to give you an assist."

"Am I under arrest?" Jack asked Konoco. He'd not gotten back in the car.

"Please ... get in," Konoco said. "No; you're not under arrest. That stupid sonofabitch!"

"Jack?" Field insisted.

"I'm fine, Mr. Speer," Jack said and got in the car.

"You need anything, give me a call!" Field shouted after the car which Konoco took out of the hotel driveway like a bat out of hell

"Fucking unbelievable!" Jack said and shook his head. "Fucking, fucking unbelievable!"

"A gay cop?" Konoco said.

Slaves

"You are a cop, then?"

"I'm am a gay cop."

"Jesus!"

"A very low-echelon cop, by the way," Konoco said. "My extended family, as many as there are of us, has never been all that trusted by the post-revolution clique. We were seen, from the start, as possibly way too friendly with the Arabs, even after slavery ended. It was only grandaddy so undeniably having once been a slave under an Arab master that saved us from the purges. Nonetheless, you'll not find any of us in genuine positions of authority."

"I've been fucked by a goddamned cop." Jack still had a hard time accepting his intuition had guided him wrong. Not that anything all that disastrous had come of it — yet.

"A horny gay cop who fucked your ass for no other reason than that he was hungry for you from the first moment he spotted you in that musty museum."

"You should have told me you were a cop," Jack said.

"Right!" Konoco said but obviously meant the opposite. He pulled the car to a stop by the apron of a side road, beneath a large tree that provided deep shade. "Paranoid as you were about even getting naked on the beach with another man, you were going to bare your ass for a known cop's cock?"

"What's with all this tourist-bureau bullshit?"

"I just happen to be a tour guide on the side," Konoco said. "You're not going to find too many people on Zanzibar who get by holding just one job. Those of us lucky enough to have two jobs still have a hard time making ends meet."

"I don't have to call in Field Speer to pull strings, then?"

"Field Speer is full of it! How do you know the bastard anyway?"

"He and I are probably the only Americans on Zanzibar, right?"

"Want to see someone up to no good, take a good look at Field Speer," Konoco said.

"What kind of no good?"

"Your guess is as good as mine, as good as anybody's, but he's up to no good, nonetheless. Why else is he back here, after all these years later."

"Back?"

"His company used to buy almost two-thirds of the total Zanzibar output of cloves, back in the days before the clove industry was taken out of Arab hands and split among so many dirt-poor locals that the whole grower-to-market pipeline got hopelessly bogged down. Field's company went elsewhere to fill his quota, and he hasn't been back since."

"Until now."

"Saying he wants to discuss resurrecting the island clove industry. The government just poor enough to give him a listen, hoping he'll provide a new influx of income, but with not a chance in hell he'll come through with a workable plan. A lot of his Arab friends, not to mention Arab business partners, were killed in the purges, and that still has Speer chewing nails."

"So, he's here on vacation. I'd think not."

"Most likely to meet dissidents, foster some kind of civil war."

"Field Speer: stereotypical rabble-rouser? Let's get real!"

"Whatever, he doesn't take three steps inside, or outside, his hotel that isn't monitored."

There was a lull in the conversation.

"You actually think I could turn you in for letting me fuck your ass?" Konoco broke the too-long silence.

"Maybe for my fucking Ahmad's ass."

"Speaking thereof, Ahmad says he's never had anyone fuck him better."

"Tell Ahmad flattery will get him everything."

Slaves

"I'm the one who wants everything," Konoco said. "Look at this dick of mine, will you?" He cupped his crotch and outlined his obviously hard cock in his pants. "Your asshole wrung it dry not all that long ago, and already it's rearing to go."

"You have a uniform?"

"Uniform?"

"That's what cops wear, isn't it? Uniforms. Even a Corporal must have a uniform."

"Maybe we once did, but no one on the force that I know can afford one."

"Pity. What gay doesn't fantasize being fucked by a cop, except to fantasize being fucked by a cop in uniform?"

"Maybe I can find someone who has one that hasn't been recycled for everyday wear."

"Maybe you'd better worry more about someone finding out about us. What we were up to in the Kidichi Baths isn't likely to put you first on any promotions list."

"All the attention focused on Speer, who's going to pay all that much attention to me or to you?" Konoco said. "Not that the rules are enforced, all that much, without Speer as a diversion. Usually, everyone on Zanzibar, including the police, has a live and let-live mentality, everyone more concerned with just surviving to see a new day."

Jack hoped Konoco was right about the degree of attention presently paid Field.

"You want me to show you just how hot and horny you make me?" Konoco said. "Show you just how sure I am that we won't be held accountable for any infraction of Zanzibar's archaic sex laws? Pull out that big cock of yours, here and now, and let me have at it."

"Christ, Konoco, we're parked along a public road! What if anyone comes by?"

"No one is going to come by," Konoco said. "Trust me.

They're all home, this time of day, too damned tired to go
anywhere after a day of trying to make a go at living on this
island. Those that have food are eating it. Those that don't
have food are conserving energy for another day of trying to
scrounge some up."

"There are people a bit more likely to have full bellies and
be on the prowl," Jack said. "The police, for instance.
Government officials, for instance."

"I know this road and the foot and auto traffic on it," Konoco
said. "You think I picked this spot at random? I picked it
because I know how well the shade masks this particular car. I
know how few people walk by or drive by at this time of day.
This stop specially chosen, because I'm starved for the taste of
your white cock and have every intention of satisfying that
hunger."

Jack checked forward and to the sides. He turned around
and looked behind. He gave confirming look-sees into each of
the available mirrors.

"This is sheer madness," Jack said but unzipped his
trousers, wanting to free his cock before its present swelling
made it too big, too stiff, and too cumbersome to pull through
the breach without a struggle.

Jack was more than a little disturbed that he, as well as
Konoco, was so hot and so horny doing what they were doing.
The seclusion and privacy of the Kidichi Baths was one thing.
This was quite another. What if someone saw them? What if
that someone wasn't nearly as liberal as Konoco, or Ahmad, or
Bonjo, as regarded gay sex? Shit could hit the fan, and the
part Jack had been paid to play in Field's ongoing operation
would be aborted, a lot of time, effort, and money flushed down
the proverbial toilet.

Knowing all of that, Jack's action once again was ruled
more by his hulky hunk of meat, tugged from the open fly of his

pants, than by his common sense. Then again, Field might even approve. Wasn't this a contact Jack cemented with a member of the local police force? Might not Konoco drop some useful information as to how Field's surveillance continued at the order of local authorities? Already, Konoco had dropped that Field, as Field had planned, had a good many people keeping track of him on a regular basis.

"Yes!" Konoco said of Jack's cock that was stiff enough to free-stand through the breach of Jack's trousers. "Let me see those big studly balls of yours, too."

In for a penny, in for a pound, Jack scooped his hand into his pants, claimed his hairy scrotum and baseball nuts, and cascaded the works over the lip of his gaping trouser fly.

Konoco tore open one of his Swedish rubbers. It was creamy white and dry, its nipple seemingly as impressive as one of Jack's nipples during orgasm but not nearly as tack-like. Konoco pinched the nipple and prepared to put the rolled condom atop Jack's dick, just as Jack's prick leaked a tear of preseminal goo.

"Jesus Christ!" Jack complained and fished his pocket for his hanky not yet completely dry from its similar mop-up in the Kidichi Baths.

"I love that goo of yours," Konoco said. "Not just because it's so sensuously slick to the touch." He dipped his forefinger into the small pond cupped within Jack's cockmouth before Jack's hanky claimed the remainder. "But because it tells me, my man, that you're just as turned on as I am. And I'm always hornier and hotter when I know the stud I'm with is appreciative of me and what I have to offer."

"There's someone, someplace, who wouldn't appreciate you and what you offer?" Jack found any such notion hard to believe. He milked his dick with his left hand and wiped the resulting drool with whatever dry spots remained on his hanky.

"Different strokes for different folks," Konoco said and waited impatiently for Jack to finish so Konoco could really begin. Konoco didn't know when he'd ever been hungrier. Not even those three days running, during a really bad stretch, when there had been nothing on the table to eat except one partially rotten banana he'd been able to salvage from a forest tree. "Some people, and I know you'll find this hard to believe, actually only like white meat."

"And don't think I'm going to start a crusade to tell them what they're missing," Jack said. "I'm quite content to have your black meat available entirely for my personal enjoyment and satisfaction."

"Except, it's your white meat that, as usual, has my attention," Konoco said, finally impatient enough to grab Jack's dick just as Jack's hanky completed drying it before its next drool.

Having the shaft of Jack's dick fisted, at least as much as he could contain within the curve of his large fingers and thumb, Konoco capped its bulbous head with the small rubber hat. He unrolled the rubber's leading edge until it slid over the flare of Jack's cockcorona and temporarily locked there. Figuring the capping capable of containing whatever the next bit of preseminal drool, Konoco swallowed Jack's big cock, from cockhead to cockroots, allowing himself the unadulterated pleasure of feeling Jack's actually naked cockshaft against his lips, against his tongue, against his inner cheeks, and against the hole of his throat.

"My God!" Jack gasped, not only appreciative of the expertise inherent in Konoco having taken all of his cock in one gagless swallow, but of the sheer novelty in having Konoco's face actually encasing the bare lower regions of Jack's stiff dick.

As Konoco had come at and over Jack's cock from the

side, Jack's dick had entered so that its back and belly slid Konoco's inner cheeks, its one side sliding the roof of Konoco's mouth, its other side sliding the black man's tongue. Konoco's nose rested with Jack's balls touching Konoco's cheek. Konoco ran a hand up Jack's leg and fondled Jack's balls and the hairy bag that contained them.

"Sweet, sweet, Jesus, sweet," Jack said. Additional, but non-verbal, response was yet more goo from his cockmouth.

At least for the moment, Jack was confident in the viability of the condom's juice-containing snugness around his cockhead, and he didn't insist Konoco withdraw, then and there, to complete the latex roll-down.

Konoco who, unlike many of his countrymen, had early heeded the warnings about AIDS and paid close attention to the exhortations of health authorities who lauded the benefits of condom use at all times, hadn't sucked even a partially naked prick in one helluva long time. So long that he couldn't remember it ever being as good as it was for him sucking Jack's cock. There was something so thoroughly sexy about the velvety soft layer of skin that wrapped the solid inner core of Jack's dick. Konoco had desperately and dangerously wanted to sample this particular prick, sans insulating rubber, ever since he'd been turned on by the sight of its bulge in Jack's pants. If Konoco wasn't crazy enough to risk an actual tasting of Jack's preseminal leakage, so close and so tempting as any potentially lethal brew disguised as Olympian ambrosia, he'd been more than prepared for this compromise that, though it didn't provide him the pleasure of sucking Jack's naked cockhead, was better than nothing.

Even as he lingered over Jack's white cock, basking in the sheer wonder of its taste, and in the way it so perfectly fit inside his face, Konoco knew he couldn't enjoy the status quo overly long. The combination of his spit, outside the rubber, and

Jack's preseminal juice inside, might eventually compromise the presently snug fit of the condom over Jack's cockcorona. Giving the naked part of Jack's dick a few final, luxurious sucks and licks, Konoco fished his pants pocket for his hanky which he used to mop his spit from the cockshaft he, inch by luscious inch, reluctantly returned to fresh air.

"We're both lucky I didn't pop my load and shoot that bit of tenuously clinging rubber down your gullet, like a cork popped from the neck of a champagne bottle," Jack said, only at that very moment aware of just how close the novelty of hot mouth around even a portion of his bare cock had him to orgasm, even more so when Konoco had been sucked all of the way down.

Konoco, who had enough of his wits still about him, to chill at the possible consequences of Jack's rubber popping free, was nonetheless excited by having taken that risk and been successful.

Konoco's mouth didn't completely free Jack's cock. It slipped up and over the turtlenecked leading edge of the condom, and anchored atop Jack's rubberized cockhead. Lips pursed tighter, Konoco's mouth again contacted the latex turtlenecking, this time from the top, and began to unroll it along the naked length of Jack's cock so recently cleaned by Konoco's spit and hanky.

Konoco's one hand still freely fondled Jack's balls and experienced the movement of those testicles within their scrotum as the hairy bag compacted to hug Jack's nuts all the better. Konoco worked his free arm between Jack's back and the car seat and held tightly to Jack's farthest hipbone.

"Jesus, fuck, Konoco!" Jack said, his hands along the Negro's neck and into Konoco's skullcap of short tight curls. "You give head to my white cock just as good as you fucked my white ass."

Slaves

If that was true, and Konoco suspected it was, it was only because Konoco went out of his way to make his sex with Jack the best sex ever. Konoco's chances of ever finding anyone sexier than this white boy, ever again, were highly unlikely. Konoco wanted all sex between Jack and him to be the ultimate in sexual satisfaction, because Konoco figured he'd be orgasming on the memories of it for many years to come. This time, when Konoco's mouth snugly encircled the base of Jack's fat cock, the entire condom, presently lost in Konoco's mouth and throat, was laid along and over the entire length and girth of Jack's erection, like plastic-wrap vacuum-packed over a very large sausage.

If Konoco missed the overt nakedness of Jack's cock, that didn't mean he wasn't excited by what he had. Just like chocolate, partially naked cock was something to be enjoyed in small doses, in order to make it special each and every time.

Konoco shook his head from side to side and let Jack's cock stir inside his mouth and throat, like a swizzle stick stirring a tall gin and tonic. He sucked down hard against the base of Jack's cock and continued that sucking until he was sure that the rubber he'd laid down remained sufficiently anchored for whatever ensuing sucks Konoco had in store for it and for the cock that rubber contained.

"Eat my white dick, you handsome black stud," Jack said, his hips reflexively providing a buck that bounced his butt on the car seat and fucked his cock more pronouncedly in and out of Konoco's continually feasting face. "Show this white boy's white dick how it's done."

Which was exactly what Konoco had in mind. If he would be forced to compare all past and future sex with this sex he enjoyed with Jack, he wanted Jack to have to do the same. Let the rich American suck and fuck, be sucked and fucked, anywhere else in the world, by white men, black men, yellow

boys, Indian chiefs, doctors, lawyers, stockbrokers, and Konoco
wanted Jack coming way from those thinking that none even
vaguely compared to sex had on Zanzibar with Konoco Fassal,
police corporal and tour-guide.

Konoco liked it down over Jack's cock as far as he could
go. Jack's crotch had a smell about it, made heavy and musky
by sex in the Kidichi Baths, by a day of heavy sweating, that
was so palatably sexy that Konoco tasted it. It not only
flavorfully played the taste buds of his tongue and filled his
nostrils, but it lingered provocatively strong within the black
pubic hair into which Konoco's nose was thrust, all of the way
down where one of Jack's muscled thighs attached to Jack's
groin.

How unkindly the circumstances that made Konoco so
attached to the cock and body of a rich white American, here
today and gone tomorrow. Why not to the black cock and black
body of a fellow poor Zanzibari, on-island for the duration? For
a blessed while, Konoco had thought the conveniently always-
available Ahmad was the best to be had. Now, cruelly, Konoco
knew the pleasure had from Ahmad's ass and from Ahmad's
cock were nothing ... nothing ... nothing ... in comparison to
what was offered by this one studly white young boy-man and
his white ass and his large white cock and his ability to respond
in kind to Konoco's sexual advances.

Jack, though, was still made too paranoid by the chances of
discovery by some passerby, being less familiar with the spot
than was Konoco, to allow Konoco to stay where he was as
long as Konoco would have liked staying there. Although
paranoia was as much an aphrodisiac, in moderate doses, as
fear could be, Jack was simply too excited to just sit there while
Konoco's mouth and throat did little more than claim Jack's
dick.

"Suck it!" Jack said, and his ass gave another reflexive

buck that would have worked his dick in Konoco's face even more if Konoco wasn't already locked so securely to the base of Jack's erection. "Come on, stud, eat my dick."

Jack's hands achieved what his butt-bounces hadn't been able to do, forcefully tugging Konoco's face up Jack's dick as far as Jack's cockhead, shoving the same face back down to Jack's balls.

"I do like that, cocksucker," Jack approved. "Like only you can do it, you sexy black bastard."

Konoco willingly complied. Not only because he was forced into it by Jack's insistence, but because he enjoyed it, was excited by it, wanted to do it, wanted to do more of it. It was what he was born to do.

"Yes," Jack complimented the enthusiasm with which Konoco joined in. "Yes, cocksucker ... oh ... Jesus ...yes!"

His lips taut, they slid up Jack's cock to Jack's knobby cockhead, where they paused, while Konoco sucked and his cheeks concaved to provide a snug vacuum whose force was felt all along the major corridor of Jack's dick to where Jack's cum securely nestled within Jack's balls.

As if Jack's scrotum were caught in the vacuum Konoco applied to the head of Jack's stiff cock, it lost even more of its remaining sag and pulled closer, ever closer, to the stalwart base of Jack's erection.

"Like only you can suck it," Jack said and pressed Konoco's head back down the uplifted hardness of Jack's cock to where Konoco snorted his pleasure into Jack's pubic hair.

Jack leaned back in his seat and used the last of his concentration, on other than his sucked cock, to be sure there were no signs of anyone reflected in any of the car mirrors. Then, he surrendered his complete attention to Konoco's increasingly intense suck of Jack's come-priming cock.

"Oh, Christ, that does feel so ... so good," Jack said. His

butt bounced on the car seat with more regularity, coordinated to best complement the bounce of Konoco's head over Jack's prick.

Konoco had sucked cocks on which he'd never really gotten the hang of it. Oh, he'd not sucked a dick yet that he couldn't coax to creaming, but there was coaxing, and then there was coaxing. Some cocks were more a job than a pleasure to blow. Not Jack's cock. God, Konoco loved sucking this white boy-man's dick!

If Konoco, a pro at sucking cock, enjoyed sucking, Jack equally enjoyed being sucked by a pro. Jack could only remember maybe two guys, out of the hundreds, more likely thousands, who had swung on Jack's dick, who had ever come close to the turn-on Konoco provided. Close not necessarily even in the same ballpark.

"Suck it! Suck it!" Jack was more and more insistent. Not that Konoco suddenly wasn't doing a good job of it. Konoco did so good a job that it was painful for Jack not to come. "Make me cream. Jesus, make me cream! Now ... now .. please, now, Konoco ... please, now!"

Konoco did as Jack asked, although he didn't know how. His sucking was no harder, no more energetic, no more coordinated, no more skillful. What it did, though, as he continued doing it, was add the final block of pleasure to a whole precariously stacked pleasure palace, critical mass achieved to explode the total structure from its inside-out.

"Oh, Christ, yes!" Jack said and groaned ecstatic appreciation of the explosion gone off inside him, funnelled to his nuts, exploded through his cock. "Take it, black ... black ... lovely black ... bastard! Take it!"

Jack's ass was airborne, lifted a good six inches off the seat, as if the explosion had occurred beneath his ass to launch him upward. His upward thrust impaled Konoco's face with every iota of cock Jack had to offer and lifted Konoco's head right along with it.

When Jack's ass collapsed back onto the seat, Konoco's face followed on down, and burrowed deeply into Jack's crotch when Jack's ass came to its sudden stop. Konoco's mouth twisted and sucked ... sucked and twisted.

Jack's cum ballooned the rubber nipple inside Konoco's throat. The cum-clogged rubber cut off Konoco's air supply, but Konoco stayed right where he was, holding his breath and sucking ... sucking... sucking.

"Fuuuuck!" Jack said and groaned as his dick, now made hypersensitive by completed orgasm, received its final mauling by Konoco's lips, mouth, and throat.

Konoco reluctantly pulled his face up the cock to free the totally empty erection. The bulbous rubber nipple, now a gelatinous nose flopped from the end of Jack's dick, didn't immediately budge but stayed locked in Konoco's throat. Konoco's fingers found the lower rim of the rubber and held it securely against the base of Jack's cock so that the stretch required by the rubber to pop its swollen rubber tip from Konoco's throat didn't slide the entire condom free to dump its hearty load.

"Empty balls," Jack said. He couldn't think of any other way to best describe the aftermath of his orgasm inside Konoco's face. "Empty ... empty ... empty ... balls."

CHAPTER 8

"It's all set," Carl's voice said over the phone line. "This Tuesday."

It was what Jack was afraid might happen, the ball suddenly rolling so fast there would be no official good-byes to Konoco who was off, somewhere, for an undetermined time, on police business. Jack had right on out and asked Konoco if the black cop's assignment had something to do with Field Speer. "Wish it did," Konoco had said. "Then, at least, I'd be in the area to say hello to you on my off-time. This is to do with a group of black marketeers we figure has been bringing in contraband from the mainland for years." There had been someone in the background insistent that Konoco get a move on. Konoco had given Jack a final, "See ya, hopefully soon!", and the line had gone dead.

"Jack?" it was Carl on this phone line.

"Tuesday? You're sure all the paperwork is in and approved?"

"You think I don't know procedure?"

"It just seems so soon. Between the request and the approval."

"Soon?" Obviously Carl, on assignment for Field far longer than Jack, had an entirely different idea of what was and wasn't soon.

"I guess I just thought it might be more complicated."

"It was plenty complicated," Carl said. "Luckily I've made a few friends over the last few months. Months," he repeated in emphasis. A reminder that, by comparison, Jack had only been on Zanzibar a few days.

"I'm delighted, Carl," Jack said with the enthusiasm he

thought warranted were the conversation overheard, were he really on Zanzibar to do a paper on the slave trade, and were he just afforded the opportunity to visit some little-known sights never frequented by tourists even in the days before there were so few tourists on the island.

"I'll pick you up early Tuesday morning," Carl said. "Five a.m. We'll want to cover a lot of territory before the advent of all the heat. Dress light. As for any equipment you'll need for the hike in, I'll bring you some of mine."

"Right."

"I've a bit of work before now and Tuesday," Carl said and, having expected far more enthusiasm, broke the communication rather abruptly.

The knock on Jack's door coincided with his replacing the receiver.

"Ferdinand, isn't it?" Jack asked, all innocence, after he'd fought the door and won it open. "Mackey?"

"Makin," Ferdinand corrected. "Do you think I might come in for a moment?"

"Sure." Jack stepped to one side. Closed the door behind them and asked, "How are the monkeys?"

"Actually, I'm not a photographer at all," Ferdinand said. Without being offered, he sat in a mildewed chair and motioned Jack to take the equally mildewed one across from him.

"I'm afraid I don't understand," Jack made stock reply.

"It's the cover story I was given when brought in by the Zanzibar government to keep an eye on Field Speer."

"I'm afraid you've lost me."

"Field Speer is on Zanzibar to do mischief."

"I thought he was here to buy cloves."

"So he says. So no one, with the exception of you, really believes. He has adequate alternative sources of cloves to meet his company's needs, hard-won after the bottom fell out of

Zanzibar clove production. He's no friend to the existing
government, not likely to come up with any plan to salvage a
derelict economy he more likely thinks the ruling clique's just
desserts, if for no other reason than because so many of his
Arab friends and business associates were fatalities of the
revolution. We think he's here to meet with subversives, even
help engineer a coup."

"Field? A freedom fighter?" Jack waited for the immediate
difference of opinion he'd expect from any true representative of
the Zanzibar government to argue the more apropos, in
Zanzibari opinion, "insurrectionist" or "guerrilla", as opposed to
the insinuation-of-a-valid-motive "freedom" fighter.

"He has lots of money," Ferdinand said instead. "A little
money goes a long way on Zanzibar these days, or haven't you
notice?"

"I have noticed," Jack agreed and waited for whatever
bullshit was to follow.

"I know you've talked to Field, both in my presence and
out," Ferdinand said.   "Believe me, I never dreamed, for
a nano-second, that he was anything other than what he said
he was, a businessman on Zanzibar to buy cloves."

"Rest assured, I'm not here to accuse you of anything.
We've checked you out and have no reason to disbelieve you're
anyone but Jack Mallard, here to do a paper on the slave
trade."

"That's a relief. But, frankly, Field involved in something
sinister boggles my mind."

"Yours, maybe. Not mine. Not the collective mind of the
Zanzibar government. Which is why I, why it, why we, need
your help."

"How can I possibly be of any help?"

"Has Field said anything to you, or to someone else within
your hearing, that may lead you to believe he's planning to

meet with any of the locals?"

"You do realize I've only seen and talked to him a very few times? It seemed the right thing to do, since we seem to be the only Americans on the island."

"Just anything he may have let slip in passing."

Jack went through his let-me-think posturing. Shook his head, but said, "Maybe something this next Wednesday."

"Oh?" Ferdinand's ears perked up so much he might have been a Vulcan.

"We were originally scheduled to do some sight-seeing," Jack lied and found it easy. "I'd mentioned my visit to the Kidichi Baths, and Field expressed an interest in seeing them, too. I'd agreed to arrange for us to go this Wednesday. Field cancelled. Said something came up."

"Any chance you might diplomatically prod him a bit, between now and Wednesday, to see if he'll be a bit more specific?"

"You think he'll come right out and tell me he's conspiring to overthrow the government?" No one really planning a coup would be so stupid.

"No, but maybe he'll give you an excuse so easily checked and found a lie that we'll know something is up."

Jack figured just such an excuse could be arranged.

"Has my little excursion with Professor Mider been cancelled, then?" Jack asked, all innocence.

That caught the Filipino bastard off guard.

"We're to leave Tuesday for three days in the field," Jack continued. "The professor is collecting additional plant specimens and has agreed to show me some slaving sites a bit off the regularly beaten paths."

"Right," Ferdinand said as if that little fact had merely escaped his mind. Any bona-fide government agent, genuinely out to enlist Jack's cooperation, would not only have known of the field trip but would have already cancelled or at least rescheduled it. "Let's wait and see what you come up with by Tuesday."

Field would be absolutely delighted to have Ferdinand harmlessly glued to him while Carl and Jack, elsewhere, got the thing done that Field really wanted done on Zanzibar.

"I can do that much for you," Jack volunteered and made it sound like playing spy was something he relished.

"You must be very careful," Ferdinand warned. "If Field thinks, for even a moment, that we've contacted you, and you've agreed to help us, he'll clam up. And that's only the least dangerous scenario."

"You mean, he might kill me?"

Ferdinand looked worried he may have scared Jack off.

"Not likely, but it's best to be extremely careful," Ferdinand said.

Jack went back into his let-me-think-about-this mode.

"Okay," Jack said finally with just, he thought, the right degree of maybe better not to get involved in this but ...

"Great!" Ferdinand said. "You can pass on to me directly anything you think pertinent. Since Field introduced us, he can't find our talking in the least suspicious."

With business seemingly completed, Ferdinand made no immediate move to leave.

"One other thing," he gave by way of explanation.

"Oh?" Jack was genuinely curious.

"I was wondering why you didn't come on over and join Bonjo and me the other evening."

Jack had to admit that was a lightning bolt from the clear blue sky.

"I really don't ..." Jack began, as if he prepared to deny it, then changed tack. "You know, it was really ..." He veered again. "I spotted you down on the beach. Thought about going down to say hello but, before I did, this black kid beat me to the punch. Thought I'd leave you two to whatever, then thought you'd spotted me and were coming on over. When you two, well, you know, didn't seem to see me but started, I'd backed myself into a corner, no quiet way out."

"That's how I pretty well had it figured," Ferdinand said.

Jack hoped that was no bullshit. If Ferdinand suspected Jack had followed the Filipino for some other reason than to come on down and say hello, this meeting got a bit more complicated.

"You were jacking off while we ... you know?" Ferdinand said.

"Afraid I couldn't help myself," Jack said. "You two were more than a little sexy, you'll have to admit."

"I like someone watching, on occasion, which was why I didn't ask you to join in when I spotted what you were up to in the adjoining bushes. Couldn't really see all that much, being as occupied as I was. But, there did seem to be something extraordinarily large in your pumping right hand."

Jack's cock started hardening in his pants. If he expected all sexual encounters to seem dull by comparison to sex with Konoco, that didn't mean he was impotent as far as any comparison possibility about to be offered.

"I see a potential problem in my being an official representative of a sexually repressed government that frowns upon such activities as those that occurred between Mr. Bonjo and I, on the night in question, while the same government isn't as likely to frown so vehemently on what you were doing that same evening. In that, I don't know of any Zanzibar statutes that deny a man his right to masturbate whenever and wherever the fancy might strike him, but as regards a black Zanzabari sucking my Filipino cock ..."

"I've heard the island's anti-gay rules aren't really enforced.

Need for foreign currency, no matter how it's got."

"I've heard that as well," Ferdinand said. "From what I've done and experienced, since I officially signed on here, I'd say that possibly is the case. However ..."

He let Jack fill in the blanks, and Jack was more than ready and willing to do so.

"Maybe the two of us can come up with something, between us, that will completely eradicate any existing fears that you may have as to my one day letting slip what I saw happen between you and Mr. Bonjo." Jack made the suggestion, because Ferdinand's anxiousness would have been reasonable if Ferdinand had been a government agent. He made it, because he felt it necessary that Konoco and/or thoughts of Konoco not entirely monopolize Jack's sex life. There had to be sex after Konoco, sex after Zanzibar, or Jack might as well retire to a solitary life in some isolated monastery.

"Why don't I let you come up with a suggestion for my possible dilemma?" Ferdinand said.

"How about you sit your ass down over my hard dick, hanging your arms from my neck, your legs wrapping my waist, your feet locking in the small of my back, like a monkey clinging for dear life to the trunk of a tree?"

Ferdinand laughed.

"That just might do the trick," the Filipino said. "Which admittedly, I might not have come up with on my own, but which I see nothing wrong with as far as following up on. It certainly would reassure me that we were brothers enough, in certain aspects of our private lives, to keep you mum about whatever you saw on the night in question."

"Let's do it, then!" Jack said and began to shed his clothes.

Ferdinand was no less quick in starting to get naked. His few seconds late start gave Jack just a bit of time to focus on what he was getting. Until now a mystery in that Jack had only glimpsed Ferdinand's hard dick in the garden-jungle.

Ferdinand naked came off decidedly boyish, although not so much that Jack, who had not, to his knowledge, fucked anyone under the age of consent, was turned off by it.

The Filipino was all naked bronze, hairless except for the patch of surprisingly uncurly pubic hair at his crotch. No real body definition. More girlish curves than masculine sharp angles, although not so girlish that Jack, who had never fucked a woman, and never intended to fuck one, was turned off by it.

Ferdinand was thin but not so thin that his bones, except for his hipbones, were thrust into any skeletal prominence. It was kind of sexy the way his flat belly concaved between his hips, punctuated dead-center by a navel that was, no argument about it, an outtie from the word go.

His cock, all six inches of it, was on its last jerks to complete erection. If Ferdinand was aware of how small his dick looked in comparison to Jack's monster, he didn't look or act it.

Ferdinand's only comments on the size of Jack's dick were, "My ass hasn't been filled quite as full in a very long time as you're obviously prepared to fill it. You might want to go slow and easy, because I'll have more trouble explaining a ripped asshole than explaining just what Mr. Bonjo and I and were ever up to. Maybe you'd consider a lubricated rubber?"

"One lubricated rubber coming up," Jack said and bent for his trousers whose front pocket held one.

"Marvellous," Ferdinand said. "Then, as soon as your cock gets latexed, it can get covered by my tight asshole as well."

As soon as the former was completed, Ferdinand wasted no time in proceeding to see the latter accomplished, also. His hands reached up and took hold behind Jack's neck. He lifted his left leg and hitched its knee so it rode Jack's right hip. With the skill of a monkey, he lifted his other leg and locked both his ankles in the small of Jack's back. Hung as he was from Jack's neck, his asscrack played hot-dog bun over the length and belly of Jack's stiff-standing wienie.

Jack's hands clamped the underhang of Filipino butt and acted as elevator mechanism to push Ferdinand up higher along Jack's torso. When Filipino asscrack slid free of Jack's cock, Ferdinand's asshole was well-aligned for taking on Jack's cock suddenly upthurst just beneath it.

"Ready to play merry-go-round horse on my phallic carrousel pole?" Jack asked.

He didn't expect any of this to be as good as his sex with Konoco, especially not as good as his sex with Konoco and Ahmad. After all, sex with two black studs had been fantasy before it had ever been reality. He'd never fantasized fucking the butt of a boyish and bronze-skinned Filipino. That didn't mean he didn't look forward to just such a fuck literally about to be dumped in his lap. Pleasure was always dolloped out one spoonful at a time, and expecting all sex to be a seven-course meal of unabashed ecstasy was expecting too much. Any sex, even the merest tidbit, could usually be counted upon to serve up enough pleasure to make it worth Jack's while.

"Ready, willing, and able," Ferdinand gave his go-ahead.

"Just keep your butt where it is while I put my dickhead directly on target," Jack said.

Jack's left hand held Ferdinand's right asscheek and maintained the upward pressure of a push. Jack's right hand pulled Jack's stiff dick out slightly from Jack's muscled belly, Jack's rubberized cockhead just barely touching Filipino asscrack directly above.

"On target," Ferdinand said when the dampness of lubricated rubber nipple tickled the opening to his behind. "You ready, stud, for the ride of your life?"

"Whenever you are," Jack said.

No sooner said than gravity and the weight of Ferdinand's ass started the slow ride of Ferdinand's anus down around Jack's cock. If Ferdinand's sphincter rolled open with comparable ease to claim Jack's cockhead, the hole beyond that doorway was mighty tight indeed.

"Mmmmmm, yes," the Filipino said and gave his ass the little wiggle that sat his rectum farther over Jack's cock.

Jack's hands cupped Ferdinand's descending asscheeks. He exerted a simultaneous outward pull along the asscrack in hopes of making the asshole a little less snug for the initial run, but he received no apparent rewards for his effort. His cock, up Ferdinand's falling ass, was a plug of sausage trying to fit casing seemingly too small to contain it.

"Tell me this isn't virgin ass," Jack said. It was very easy, as boyish as Ferdinand looked, to imagine the Filipino fucked for the very first time.

"Like my tight ass, do you, stud?" Ferdinand asked. "I thought that you would. Just as I thought I'd like your big cock stuck up it. Going to like it even better when I start bouncing my asshole over your dick like a kid bouncing a pogo stick."

Ferdinand's ass reached bottom, his asscheeks snugly placed against what would have been Jack's lap if Jack had been seated. Filipino balls would have touched Jack's belly, except Ferdinand's nuts were cascaded in the opposite direction. The six inches of Ferdinand's erect cock provided a baby obelisk in the space between two firm stomachs.

"Ready, American cowpoke — or should I say buttpoke — for the ride of your life?"

"Giddyap!" Jack said.

"Ride 'em, cowboy!" Ferdinand said and commenced a buck on Jack's cock that proved, once and for all, that his ass might seem virgin, but it had been showcased at more than a few other sexual rodeos before this one.

Using his leg muscles, and the hold he still had on Jack's neck, Ferdinand did most of the work. Jack's hands, still clamped to the underside of Ferdinand's ass, and Jack's cock, thrust deeply up Filipino anus, were merely along for the ride.

Jack widened his stance for better balance. He thought briefly of walking Ferdinand's back to the nearest wall, but he decided against it for fear it would interfere with the rhythm Ferdinand had so easily and quickly achieved. So, Jack just stood, let Ferdinand's efforts work their magic in elevating Jack's big nuts. Jack waited for Ferdinand, all by his lonesome, to swell either or both of their pleasure to inevitable orgasmic overflow.

"Done this before, haven't you?" Jack said. The counterweight of Ferdinand's hung body allowed Jack to lean backwards in a way that levered his hips forwards and upwards to provide his cock additional depth and penetration of the Filipino's bucking ass.

"You can always tell a pro from an amateur, can't you, cowboy?" Ferdinand took credit where credit was due. "Just by what little I saw of you manhandling your dick off the beach, that one night, I could tell that you and your dick would really know how to give a guy a good time."

No way could Jack believe that Ferdinand got more pleasure than the Filipino was giving. If Jack couldn't help the comparison of this sex with sex had with Konoco and Ahmad, to judge this sex the inferior, it was good enough to get the job done. Jack hadn't experienced an orgasm yet that he didn't enjoy, and he had no doubts that he'd enjoy this one.

"You want me to try and play with your dick?" Jack asked, figuring he might be able to get hold of Ferdinand's cock as erected between them.

"I think you're going to be surprised by how well my dick can take care of itself, my butt with a really nice-sized hunk of meat working piston-like inside it," Ferdinand said. "You just relax and let the two of us enjoy. My enjoyment only made better in knowing now, for certain, that you're too much a brother in butt-fucking to spill to the Zanzibar authorities my penchant for fucking the occasional black mouth."

"My only spilling is going to be hot and heavy cream," Jack said by way of warning that his cock would have to be dead not to be responding, hard and fast, to Ferdinand's nonstop, rip-roaring ride on it. He tried to slow Ferdinand's bounce, just a tad, by taking a firmer handhold of Filipino ass, but it really didn't do that much good.

Ferdinand commenced a series of laybacks, his arms fully extended, on each complete positioning of Jack's cock up his butt. Ferdinand began leaving his ass all the way down for a few seconds longer than usual, grinding it over and around the base of Jack's sticking erection. Then, his elbows bending, Ferdinand pulled his chest and belly back into Jack's chest and belly for the slide of his ass back up Jack's cock to Jack's cockhead. Only to repeat the process again ... again ... again.

Jack began reflexive bounces that flexed and unflexed his legs at his knees, providing staccato pokes up and back of his ass-swallowed and ass-released inches.

The heat and humidity of the room, the heat and humidity of the fuck, glossed the bodies of both young men with an attractive lacquer-finish of sweat. Ferdinand seemed more bronze, Jack more golden. They presented the illusion of two erotic metal statues, thrust together in a fiery furnace, steadily increasing heat melting and melding them into one passion-wrought amalgamate.

"Fuuuuuck ... it!" Jack said every time Ferdinand's ass reached bottom and commenced its few seconds of grinding that demanded Jack's orgasm manifest itself all the sooner.

"Feels like I've got your dick rammed all the way up my

butt, all the way through my belly, all the way into the base of my throat," Ferdinand said next time he sat the total length of Jack's upstanding dick.

"You ready for a butt full of cum-ballooned rubber?" Jack asked on Ferdinand's next butt lift, only Jack's cockhead once again securely gummed by Filipino sphincter.

"My butt has been ready since I first spotted you in the hotel bar," Ferdinand assured.

After which, neither did any conscious talking, their every effort more and more concentrated on bringing their pleasure to a mutually sought and desired conclusion. If they made sounds — guttural sounds, animalistic sounds, sighs, pants, gargles — it was all reflexive, automatic response to a wave of combined pleasure that had built so high as to begin the curl that would soon crash down upon both of them.

The explosion went off in the pit of Jack's belly with such force that it seemed the final upward ride of Ferdinand's butt was the direct result of Jack's orgasm supplying the launching. So hard and so fast was the condom nipple pumped full of Jack's exploded cream, up Filipino ass, that the ballooned results temporarily lodged tightly within the corridor of Ferdinand's anus and, had Ferdinand's ass been totally blasted free of Jack's cock, then and there, would have taken the rubber along with it, leaving Jack's naked cock to drool any additional cream. For a minute, the splash of wet-warm cum across Jack's chest and his belly had him thinking that was exactly what had happened. Only, it was Ferdinand's naked six inches of hard cock that erupted, having needed only the constant glide of Jack's hard cock within Filipino butt to pull their trigger.

CHAPTER 9

On Monday, Jack told Ferdinand that Field apparently had a Wednesday afternoon meeting with a local businessman who supposedly had a museum-quality antique scimitar to sell. It was a lie, but Field was prepared to give it the appearance of clandestine possibility by taking a cab to the old city, come Wednesday afternoon, to wander the bazaar and, thereby, hopefully, keep Ferdinand in tow and out of mischief.

On Tuesday, Carl Mider left on his field trip, Jack in tow. By Wednesday morning, they had left the car behind and hiked deep into the countryside. By Wednesday afternoon, Field lazily examining a pile of coconuts in the marketplace of the old city, Carl and Jack reached Field's real objective in the interior of the island.

Carl had been on site before. He'd been sent to Zanzibar specifically to locate it, based upon disjointed segments of information that had managed to get out of Zanzibar during the revolution that had deposed long-standing Arab influence.

Both his first and second nights in the field with Carl, Jack expected sex. He was ready for it. The sudden race toward culmination of the project for which both men had been hired was something Jack found sexually stimulating. However, Carl, longer subjected to the traumas of the project, was made impotent by the potential catastrophe that could yet occur, even at this late date, if it were discovered what Jack and Carl, at the Field's instigation, were up to.

Carl wouldn't have been the first limp-dicked guy Jack had ever fucked, if Carl had been willing, but Carl had become the exact opposite of the sexually aggressive satyr he'd been at Jack and his encounter at the museum.

– 127 –

Slaves

Jack might have attempted seduction, but he was really too tired from hiking the Zanzibar wilderness to bother. He wasn't too tired to jack-off, though. Carl's only comment, upon hearing Jack masturbate, was something to the effect that everyone might have been better served if Jack conserved his energy for what was yet left for him to do after Carl was finished — finally — with Carl's part of the project.

Jack, though, had Thursday morning to rest, while Carl busied himself with his area of expertise. Jack watched fascinated as Carl proved his worth in having been bought and paid for. In the end, the payload, succinctly packaged in a carrying case and fitted into a backpack, was less a discomfort than the heat of the day in which Jack was required to carry it.

"You know what to do," Carl said. To have come this far, this close to success, only to have Jack, good in bed definitely, good as a courier yet to be seen, screw up would have been a capital-punishment offense, as far as Carl was concerned.

"Got it, Professor!" Jack said, backpack on. He hoped Carl now wanted sex, just so Jack could say no. Sex, though, remained the farthest thing from Carl's mind.

"Well, then," Carl said and checked his watch. "I trust you've memorized the timetable."

"Funny, but I don't once remember questioning whether or not you were up to your part in all of this deal."

"I'm sorry," Carl said. "Really. It's just that I've devoted so much of the last couple of years to get to this point that I hate to think it can still end up coming to nothing."

"I'll do my part," Jack assured, although the show was never over until the fat lady sang.

Their parting handshake was anticlimactic, considering the heated sex that had once passed between them.

Jack took a visual sighting off the seemingly ever-present sun and headed into the underbrush. Somewhere ahead was the ocean, and the boat supposedly put in place by other Field employees as Jack and the payload's ticket out of there. No boat would cause possible catastrophic repercussions for the fragile cargo that now counted upon its quick delivery to the people best qualified to preserve it.

As had been the case in the hotel's garden-jungle, Jack heard the ocean before he saw it. So much before that he decided, more than once, it wasn't the ocean at all but merely the wind through the trees.

It was actually sunset by the time he crested the hill and saw the expanse of salt water that separated him from the African mainland.

Miraculously, he spotted the row of palms, two made all the more phallic by having been decapitated by some storm, or maybe by disease.

"A little closer to success, by the minute," Jack complimented himself, adjusted the load on his back, and headed for his hopefully awaiting transportation.

"Chock up one more success to Field's deep pockets," Jack said, on site, when he'd removed a couple of the dried palm fronds to reveal a promising segment of boat underneath.

Only to feel the sharp pain at the back of his head and lose all sense of anything except all-encompassing darkness.

He awoke to the realization that somebody was busy fucking the shit out of him.

Jack had had cock fucked up his butt enough times to know what it felt like and to know that the cock working his asshole was a big one. No mistaking the weight of someone laid along his back and ass; the guy's arms looped under Jack's arms; the guy's hands looped up, over, and locked at the nape of Jack's neck in a full nelson. Jack's face turned to the left. Against his cheek something soft like a blanket.

Either the blow to his head had rendered him blind, or he

was blindfolded. Either he was mute, or he as gagged. Either he was paralyzed, or he was tied, face-down, and spread-eagled.

He jerked his arms and heard the distinct rattle of chains, even over his molester's grunts that were loud and guttural in Jack's ears. Obviously, Jack's hearing remained in A-one condition.

The cock that worked Jack's butt did so at such a speed, the accompanying grunts of its owner so frequent and breathy, the fuck, obviously begun while Jack was unconscious, had continued for some time before Jack recovered. Whoever had screwed Jack's unconscious ass to consciousness still had himself one helluva good time.

It wasn't his rape that so much bothered Jack. After all, he'd had cock up his butt before, thrust into him far more painfully, in fun and games, than this cock managed in uninvited sex. What Jack found a worse scenario was that Jack's attacker might not have had the forethought to wear a rubber. If Jack concentrated to determine if it was rubberized dick up his butt, it was impossible for him to tell at this stage of the game. He could only hope this big-cocked stud had been fearful enough, for his own safety, to sock his dick before sticking it up Jack's asshole

After convincing himself that only a fool, in this day and age, would shove unprotected cock up any funky asshole, without first knowing the medical and sexual history of the butt's owner, Jack found disconcerting the hardness of his own cock beneath his own belly. Since he didn't remember it getting that way, it had erected reflexively, while Jack was unconscious, stiffened by whatever subconscious sensations Jack had received once the rapist's cock had plugged in and set to work.

If ever Jack wanted the Zanzibar authorities to arrive on the scene and nab someone breaking Zanzibar sex laws, he

wanted them to nab this guy riding Jack's ass. Except Jack
might end up having to make embarrassing explanations, for
which he had none, as to why he had such a rip-roaring boner
as a result of some cock thrust in and out of his asshole.

Rapes more about power than about sex, Jack was taken
by the notion that the stud who rode him might not get such a
bang out of what he did if he knew his victim wasn't having that
much of a bad time.

The next time the cock shot deep up Jack's asshole, Jack
provided a sensuous rotation of his hips. Jack knew, from long
experience, that such a roll could provide more fucking pleasure
than just keeping to a straight in and out jabbing of penis up
asshole. He was tremendously pleased when his assailant
grunted immediate response and there was an obvious, albeit
short, glitch in the fucking rhythm.

Jack attempted a hopefully more give-me-more than an oh-
no-please-no-more groan. He was prepared to try another but
was distracted by how the shifting weight of his fucker caused
the shifting of Jack's belly that caused Jack's cock to shift
against the underlying blanket. Jack's cock, for Christ's sake!,
having already leaked enough preseminal juice, actually
screwed a bubbly cocoon of its own making.

"Aaagghhruungh!" Jack's groaned, this time because of
pleasure real not faked.

Suddenly, even the way Jack rattled his chains became an
auditory aphrodisiac.

Suspecting something a bit perverted about getting off on
his butt being raped, Jack concentrated on keeping his pleasure
at bay. He didn't much succeed, not even when he focused on
the pain in the back of his head from the blow received.

He felt some confidence that his assailant's head start
would see the rapist creaming long before Jack's nuts were
adequately primed.

Jack really felt proud of himself when the cock exploded up his butt. Not so proud of himself when the resulting ripplings of pleasure funnelled immediately into Jack's balls.

"Shit, no, no, shit!" Jack protested, although it didn't come out around his gag sounding anything like that.

His hard cock squirted cum beneath his belly, and his asshole clamped so tightly, as a result, that Jack's rider squealed a combination pleasure/pain because of the sudden anal mauling of his dick made hypersensitive by having already blasted. When the cock slipped free of Jack's asshole, Jack waited for what came next, his senses narrowed to what he could feel and hear.

He still experienced pain from the blow that had been delivered to the back of his head, although it wasn't as painful as Jack thought it should be. He felt the cooling mess of his cum beneath his jism-smeared belly, although he preferred ignoring it, because he hadn't yet decided if someone knocked unconscious and raped should have enjoyed it quite as much.

He heard the crackle of a possible campfire. He heard his attacker, or maybe an accomplice, up and moving. He heard two distinct clicks that he attributed to the latches being released on the special container that had been carried in on Jack's back.   "Don't!" Jack tried to tell the bastard. A novice, who didn't have a clue, could do irreparable damage to the goods, make them virtually unsalvageable, and they were presently ones of a kind.

Quite unexpectedly, two hands were placed beneath Jack head to turn Jack's face in the opposite direction. Jack's gag was pulled free, his blindfold removed with equal informality.

While Jack greeted what was still obviously a Zanzibar after-dark, the light from the campfire was enough to disorient him until his eyes adjusted to the flickering flames. By that time, his assailant had moved into view and seated himself,

specimen case open on a rock in front of him, a cum-filled
rubber dangling from the pinch of his forefinger and thumb.

"Just so you know I wasn't stupid enough to fuck you
without a rubber," he said.

"Konoco?" Jack's mouth hadn't adjusted to having been
gagged. Jack recognized what he said,but it wasn't likely
Konoco had made heads or tails of it.

"You want to tell me what these are, Jack?" Konoco said,
and nodded toward the open case from which one sample had
been removed. He tossed the cum-drooped rubber to one side.
"Or, do you want me to tell you what they are and what brings
you and them to this supposedly deserted part of the island?"

"You've been spying on me from the start!" Jack accused.

"Don't be such a fucking asshole! I wouldn't have made the
connection on a bet."

"But ..."

"A local fisherman spotted the boat and reported it.
Everyone suspecting black-marketeers. Since I'm low man on
the totem pole, I got assigned to stand watch out here in the
boondocks. Who could have guessed this really involved
probably the only things left on this island worth the risk of
smuggling out?"

"I really wish you'd put that specimen back in its carrying
case. It, and its companions, were packed specifically to
remain where they were even when checked to be sure they
weren't drying out."

"Tell me these aren't cuttings and grafts from the rumored
super clove."

"Those aren't cuttings and grafts from the rumored super
clove," Jack obliged.

"Liar! One of Field's Arab friends actually found one before
the purge."

Konoco obviously knew what he had.

Slaves

"Found just at the onset of the revolution," Jack admitted. "Word of it so fragmented by the time it got to Field that he needed years to feel confident he had actually pinpointed the exact locale."

"Carl Mider sent in to verify. Who else but a botanist, for Christ's sake! You one, too?"

"Just a lowly courier."

"I should have known you were too damned good to be true."

"Any of this makes me less good?"

"What's the eugenol yield from this botanical mutant?" Konoco ignored Jack's attempt at humor. "One-hundred percent over normal? Two-hundred percent?"

"The conservative estimate: Six-hundred-ninety-point-nine percent."

"Enough to put Zanzibar back on the map, if it started cultivating such a super clove en masse, wouldn't you say?"

"I'd say the system presently in place is no more geared to exploit this potential than it was to maintain pre-revolutionary output of cloves after the revolution. Nationalization of the clove industry what shot the industry all to shit. That's changed, has it?"

"All of which gives Field, so much money already that it's coming out of his ass, the right to make even more money?"

"Field owned a seventy-five percent stake in the plantation on which this clove was found and never received one cent of reparation from the Zanzibar government when the plantation was seized, Arab overseers killed. Field merely seeing this as a long-term return on his original investment, as well as his return on additional monies spent to get what he considers to be his own property this far."

"What's your share of this clove pie?"

Jack halved his take, halved it again, remembered how

financially strapped Zanzibar was, and opted for an even lower figure yet. It was still more than Konoco could hope to see in his lifetime on the island.

"Who knows I'm here?" Jack asked in follow-up. "Besides you."

"You don't think my knowing isn't plenty enough for you to worry about?"

"You could come with me."

"Right! Zanzibar police corporal disappears with missing American tourist. I've got an extended family here that doesn't need the extra shit that'll come from me suddenly labelled a suspected co-conspirator, kidnapper, or fuck-up. On the other hand, I could turn you and these cuttings and grafts over to my superiors and possibly reap some kind of reward."

"You mean, a slap on the back while your superiors think how they make the big money off this? All the while, without proper supervision, the cuttings and grafts having their valuable viability compromised by even more mishandling."

"Aren't you forgetting the Mother Lode still out there? Clove trees grow exceptionally big, given time, and this super clove tree has had a good many years to do just that."

"Except, Mama's dead, isn't she? Carl killed her with an overdose of chemical growth stimulizer. Once Field had the legitimate heirs, he couldn't risk the Queen or any of her bastards someday usurping the throne, could he?"

Konoco replaced the cutting and its containing vial back into the slot designed specifically for it within the well-padded carrying case. He closed the case lid and affixed the latches. He shifted his full attention back to Jack and untied him.

"Get dressed," Konoco said.

"Help me, and Field will make it worth your while," Jack said.

Slaves

"I'm surprised it took you so long to get around to that most obvious solution," Konoco said.

"You'll have to act fast, though, so as many cuttings and grafts as possible survive the interruption."

"I was fast," Konoco said. He was disappointed to see all Jack's sexy masculinity, big cock, and sexy ass, once again concealed behind clothing. "As soon as it became blatantly obvious to me what you were up to here, I called a cousin who works at your hotel, who contacted Field who, after doing his paranoia act, decided to cut the possibility of total loss by making my cooperation financially worth my while. You might be interested to know, by the way, that because of our past relationship, I had Field told that none of this was your fault. Just a fluke. Nine times out of ten, the fisherman who'd spotted your getaway boat would have hauled it off and made it his own."

"Thanks."

"I did it for the good times, Jack. We did have some of those, didn't we?"

"The best."

"We'd better get moving," Konoco said and got to his feet. "We've a good deal of ground to cover, and I have to get back here before my superiors check in to see if I've spotted any signs of black-marketeers yet."

It was a forced march accomplished more quickly by Konoco and Jack taking turns with the pack. They arrived, five minutes after midnight, at a beach Jack found not all that different from the one they'd left cross-country.

"I've an uncle whose fishing boat passes here every morning," Konoco said. "Regular as clockwork. Just before dawn, he'll send a dinghy for you."

He squatted beside Jack who had collapsed to get his breath.

"You know, everyone always heard the rumors of this super clove, but no one really believed it existed. While everyone, including me, did believe Field here to meet with dissidents and finance revolution. The irony being that Field ends up financing a revolution after all. You know how many guns, and how much ammunition, can be bought with the money he's paying me to get you and these botanical scraps off this island?"

"You're going to foment revolution?"

"Would you want to live under conditions you've seen here, under a regime so oppressive that two queers can't fuck or suck in the privacy of their own bedrooms without there being a law against it?"

"Revolution is dangerous."

"Danger an aphrodisiac, right?"

Konoco stood.

"Think of me sometime, won't you, Jack?" He headed off the way they'd come.

"You know, Konoco," Jack called after, "you really owe me a fuck for the one taken back there without asking."

"Yeah, I know," Konoco said, stopping momentarily but not turning back. "And I expect you to demand payback, with compound interest, the next time you're on Zanzibar."

He proceeded into the night.

Jack waited a few minutes then unzipped his pants. He hauled out his stiff prick and immediately started beating it. Each hearty stroke of his fist over his dick had him fantasizing the same thing he would fantasize for years to come. Sometimes while beating his own meat. Sometimes while in bed with a real loser. Sometimes while in bed with someone as studly as he was. Always, though, the fantasy of Jack's hard, white, steely dick ramming ... ramming ... ramming ... Konoco Fassal's tight, black, squirming ass.